We Will Have Better Days

BY

BRENDAN LARKIN

MAPLE

PUBLISHERS

We Will Have Better Days

Author: Brendan Larkin

Copyright © 2025 Brendan Larkin

The right of Brendan Larkin to be identified as the author of this work has been asserted by the author in accordance with section 77 and 78 of the Copyright, Designs and Patents Act 1988.

ISBN 978-1-83538-713-9 (Paperback)
978-1-83538-714-6 (Hardback)
978-1-83538-715-3 (E-Book)

Book layout and cover design by:
Maple Publishers
www.maplepublishers.com

Published by:
Maple Publishers
Fairbourne Drive, Atterbury,
Milton Keynes,
MK10 9RG, UK
www.maplepublishers.com

A CIP catalogue record for this title is available from the British Library.

For Mum.

Your love was my first story.

This book is for you.

About the Author
Brendan BS Larkin

Brendan Larkin is a Galway man with a deep-rooted passion for storytelling. Growing up in the West of Ireland, Brendan was shaped by the rhythms of country life, the warmth of community, and the rich oral traditions that echoed through the towns and villages. His stories are steeped in the culture and spirit of his homeland, blending lyrical prose with an instinctive understanding of human nature.

Whether crafting tales of quiet introspection or sweeping sagas of adventure, Brendan brings a keen eye for detail and a heart full of empathy to every page. His voice is unmistakably Irish, earthy, poetic, and alive with the cadence of a storyteller who knows his roots and speaks from the soul.

When he's not writing, Brendan can often be found exploring the landscapes that inspire him, from the winding streets of Galway City to the rural countryside and its beauty.

Introduction

In the rugged beauty of the West of Ireland, where the wild Atlantic crashes against ancient cliffs and the fields are stitched together by weathered stone walls, life is a tapestry of tradition, struggle, and fleeting joy. The year is 1913, and the winds of change are blowing through the quiet villages and rolling hills, carrying with them whispers of rebellion and the promise of a free Ireland.

For Alice Duffy, an only child, life has always been bound by the rhythms of the land and the expectations of her community. But when she falls in love with Jimmy, a farm hand, her world is turned upside down. Their love will bring them to the edge.

When Alice discovers she is pregnant, she faces a world quick to judge and slow to forgive. Cast out by tradition and fear of being placed in a mother and baby home she must find the strength to forge her own path in a land as unyielding as its people. Jimmy, meanwhile, is not able to be with her.

Set against the backdrop of the Great War, the Easter Rising, and the War of Independence, this is a story of resilience and rebellion, of love tested by hardship and hope forged in the crucible of struggle. In the face of heartbreak and betrayal, Alice and Jimmy must navigate a world where personal dreams and the Church collide, and where the fight for a new Ireland mirrors their fight for a future together.

In this tale of the West, where the land and the people share a history of endurance, love is both a refuge and a battlefield, and every choice carries the weight of a nation yearning to be free.

Characters

- Pete Flaherty
- Kate Flaherty
- Connor Flaherty
- Mol Flaherty
- Pat Flaherty

- Alice Duffy
- Jimmy White
- James

- Coleman Casey
- Eve White
- Sarah White

- Father Michael
- bishop in Galway
- bishop in America
- Kieran and Denny Moran
- Joe
- Sergeant Brown
- Sister Tessa
- Maureen
- Kathleen
- Cis

Pete Flaherty

Pete was born into a family of tenant farmers, enduring a childhood marked by poverty and relentless toil. His father, a man broken by both the land and British landlords, instilled in Pete the belief that survival depended on unyielding hard work. After his father's death, Pete took over the farm at just 17, determined to transform it into a self-sustaining legacy for his family.

In 1908, Pete secured ownership of the farmland under the Land Act, a hard-won victory that further cemented his belief in the redemptive power of labour. For him, the land symbolised survival, pride, and duty.

Pete was stoic, practical, and unrelenting in his principles. He valued work above all else, often to the detriment of his relationships. His love for his family was buried beneath a gruff exterior, expressed more in the food on the table and the roof over their heads than in words or tenderness.

Pete was a tall, wiry man with calloused hands and a face weathered by years of exposure to wind and sun. His clothes, though patched, were always clean. He walked with a slight limp, a relic of an injury sustained while clearing stones from a field

Beneath his hardened exterior, Pete carried guilt and a buried longing for the warmth he could not show his children. His own childhood was devoid of affection, and he knew no other way, he sometimes wonders if his father's approach was the only path. He feared being seen as weak, but in quiet moments, he questioned whether he raised his children with too heavy a hand.

Kate Flaherty

Kate grew up in a modest but lively household where music, storytelling, and laughter balanced the hard work of daily life. Her father was a schoolteacher, and her mother took pride in keeping a warm, welcoming home. Kate dreamed of a life that blended comfort with connection, a home where family could gather, talk, and find solace after a long day.

She married Pete at 21, drawn to his quiet strength and determination. In their early years, Pete's softer side shone through in small gestures, a wildflower tucked into her apron, a rare but heartfelt compliment, or a shared laugh over a pot of tea. Over time, however, the weight of the farm and Pete's unyielding work ethic hardened him, leaving Kate yearning for the warmth they once shared.

Kate was patient, proud, and resourceful. She kept the household running with meticulous care, taking pride in the details, especially her parlour, a sanctuary of order and charm in a world of relentless labour - a quiet, nurturing woman who acted as a buffer between Pete and their children. While outwardly stoic, she felt deeply, holding onto quiet hopes that Pete might one day soften again. She's skilled at reading people and adept at creating moments of calm amid chaos.

Kate had a graceful, understated beauty. Her hair, once jet black, was streaked with grey, often swept into a neat bun. Her hands were roughened by work but always clean. She took care to wear her best shawl when visiting neighbours and maintained an air of dignity despite their modest means.

Kate's parlour was her pride and joy, a space she kept immaculately clean and decorated with her mother's lace doilies, a polished brass lamp, and a small vase of wildflowers of the season. Though rarely used, it's her symbol of hope and a testament to the life she imagined when she first became a wife.

Kate felt torn between her loyalty to Pete and her longing for a more affectionate marriage. She sometimes wondered if she had done enough to help Pete carry his burdens or if she had simply been left behind in his pursuit of survival. Quietly, she dreamt of rekindling the spark between them, but she didn't know how to reach the man he's become.

Connor Flaherty

Connor Flaherty was a tall, broad-shouldered young man of 19, with a wiry build honed by long days working on his family's farm in the rugged countryside of County Galway, Ireland. His tousled dark hair fell over a sun-bronzed face, marked by a strong jaw and bright green eyes that reflected both the wild beauty of his homeland and his own untamed spirit. His smile was warm and disarming, a testament to his kind and gentle nature.

Connor was deeply connected to the land he grew up on, cherishing the rolling hills and windswept fields of his village. Despite his humble beginnings, there's a restless energy in him, a longing for more than the life his father has led. Ambitious and forward-thinking, Connor dreamt of finding a way to improve the lives of his family and neighbours, perhaps even beyond the borders of Ireland. His kindness extended to everyone he meets; he's quick to lend a hand and is known for his generosity and an unwavering sense of fairness.

While his heart is tied to the traditions of his home, Connor was not afraid to challenge the status quo. His ambition fueled his desire to learn and explore, and though his dreams sometimes seemed out of reach, his determination and charm inspired those around him to believe in a brighter future.

Mol Flaherty

Mol Flaherty was a fiery and determined young woman of 21, with an air of quiet intensity that belies her rural upbringing. Slightly shorter than her brother Connor, she carried herself with a commanding presence that makes her seem taller. Her auburn hair, often tied back to keep it out of her way while working, often caught the sunlight in fiery streaks, complementing her pale, freckled complexion. Her sharp, grey eyes pierced through any pretence, reflecting her keen intellect and unyielding resolve.

As the eldest daughter in the Flaherty family, Mol spent much of her life balancing farm chores with a relentless hunger for knowledge. She was known in the village for her quick wit and fierce independence, often debating with the local men about politics and the future of Ireland. While others seen her as stubborn, she viewed her defiance as necessary in a world where women's voices were often dismissed.

Mol's ambition goes far beyond the boundaries of her family's farm. She dreamt of a free Ireland, unshackled from British rule, and seen the fight for independence as her calling. She spent evenings reading anything she can find about Irish history and politics. Her cleverness allowed her to navigate the delicate line between speaking her mind and avoiding trouble with the authorities, though she had no fear of facing danger for her beliefs.

Beneath her fierce exterior, Mol carried a deep love for her family and her homeland. Her passion for freedom was rooted in a desire to create a better future for her siblings and for the generations to come. Mol Flaherty was a force to be reckoned with, a woman whose ambition burned as brightly as her fiery hair.

Pat Flaherty

Pat Flaherty, the youngest child of the Flaherty family at 17, was a stark contrast to his siblings. He was a lanky, somewhat unkempt young man with a mop of dark, messy hair that he seldom bothered to tame. His pale complexion hinted at his preference for staying out of the sun whenever possible, and his blue eyes, though sharp, often carried a sleepy or disinterested look.

Unlike his ambitious brother Connor or his fiery sister Mol, Pat was content to let life unfold around him with minimal effort on his part. He's often found lounging in the shade while others toil in the fields, absently whittling a piece of wood or idly tossing stones. Though he's capable of hard work, when necessary, he approached tasks with a begrudging attitude, doing only what's required to avoid a scolding from his father.

Pat dreamt of an easy, carefree life far from the endless chores of the farm and the heated discussions of Irish politics that dominate the household. He had no desire to be a hero or a revolutionary; instead, he imagined a future where he can enjoy life's comforts without much struggle, perhaps a job in a shop or a chance to marry into a family with a bit of money.

Despite his laziness, Pat had a charm that endears him to some in the village, particularly the older women who chuckle at his quick-witted excuses for dodging work. He had a sly sense of humour and a knack for talking his way out of trouble, though this only fuelled his reputation as a dreamer unwilling to shoulder responsibility.

Pat might have lacked the drive and determination of his siblings, but he had a certain easy-going charisma. Beneath his laziness lay a cunning streak, hinting that, while he avoided effort, he actively sought a comfortable life.

Alice Duffy

Alice Duffy was an 18-year-old cottager's daughter with quiet strength and an unassuming grace that reflected her simple yet resilient upbringing in the West of Ireland. Slender and petite, with delicate features, she had pale skin that flushes easily and dark, wavy hair often tied in a loose braid. Her large, deep brown eyes carried a softness that drew people in, but beneath their gentle gaze lay a quiet determination.

Alice was known in her small village for her kind and empathetic nature. She often helped her mother care for their modest home, tending to their small garden and looking after her younger siblings. Despite the hardships of her family's life, she found joy in simple pleasures, singing folk songs while she worked, gathering wildflowers, and sharing stories by the fire.

Though Alice appears reserved, she had a sharp mind and a keen awareness of the world around her. She was observant and thoughtful, often surprising those who underestimated her with her perceptive insights. She longed for more than the life of a cottager but was realistic about the limitations placed on her by her station and the times she lived in.

Alice had a strong sense of loyalty and pride in her heritage, and while she didn't possess the fiery revolutionary spirit of someone like Mol Flaherty, she supported the dream of an independent Ireland in her own quiet way. She admired bravery and ambition in others, and her heart harboured dreams of a brighter future, perhaps one where she might have stepped beyond the constraints of her upbringing and find her own path.

Alice Duffy's gentle demeanour and steadfast resilience made her a grounding presence for those around her. While she may not have had the loudest voice in the room, her kindness and quiet strength left a lasting impression on all who know her.

Jimmy White

Jimmy White was a 20-year-old cottager's son with an infectious energy that lit up any room he enters. He was of average height but stocky and strong from years of farm labour, with a ruddy complexion that hinted at his time spent outdoors. His short, sandy-blond hair was always slightly dishevelled, and his bright blue eyes sparkled with mischief and good humour. His broad grin, could have lifted the spirits of even the gloomiest soul.

Jimmy was known throughout the village for his kind heart and his natural gift for making others laugh. Whether it's through a well-timed joke, a light-hearted story, or a cheerful song, he had a knack for bringing people together and easing tensions. He's the kind of man who would lend a hand to anyone in need, no questions asked, and expects nothing in return but a smile and maybe a bottle of stout at the local pub.

While Jimmy didn't harbour grand ambitions like some of his peers, he was fiercely loyal to his friends, family, and his community. He had a deep love for Ireland and its traditions, though he's more interested in preserving the joy and camaraderie of village life than getting involved in political causes. That said, his trustworthy nature and unshakable optimism made him someone people naturally look to in times of trouble.

Jimmy was also a bit of a romantic, with a soft spot for music and storytelling. He often dreamt of a life where he could settle down, raise a family, and share his love of simple joys with those around him. His good will and easy-going charm made him beloved by all, from the local children who adored his antics to the elders who appreciated his respectful and sunny disposition.

In a world often filled with hardship, Jimmy White was a beacon of warmth and positivity, embodying the spirit of a man who believed life was meant to be shared, celebrated, and lived with an open heart.

Father Michael

Father Michael was a man in his late 50s, with a rotund figure and an air of authority that loomed larger than his actual stature. His thinning grey hair was slicked back, and his sharp, dark eyes seemed to scrutinise everyone he met, as though measuring their usefulness to his ambitions. His round, ruddy face often carried a stern expression, though it could have quickly morphed into façade of piety when needed.

Draped in the austere black robes of his office, Father Michael projected the image of a devout and disciplined clergyman. However, beneath this façade lay a man driven by cunning and greed. He used his position as the parish priest to manipulate the faithful, ensured their loyalty not through genuine care or guidance but through fear of divine retribution and the strict dictates of the Church.

Father Michael was known for his sharp tongue and his ability to twist any situation to his advantage. He demanded generous donations from his impoverished flock, often citing the Church's needs while lining his own pockets. Whispers circulated in the village about his dealings with wealthier landowners, and it's said that he was quick to turn a blind eye to injustice if it benefitted him.

Despite his lack of genuine care for his parishioners, Father Michael was skilled at maintaining his image. He delivered fiery sermons that kept the villagers in line and ensured his authority went unchallenged. His cunning allowed him to navigate any conflict, using scripture and his position to silence dissent and deflect criticism.

Father Michael's presence cast a shadow over the community, a reminder of the power wielded by the Church in rural Ireland. Though many feared him, a few dared to openly question him, for he was a master of using guilt and the weight of religious dogma to maintain control. For Father Michael, faith was less about spirituality and more about leverage, a means to secure his own comfort and authority at the expense of those he was meant to serve.

Coleman Casey

Constable Coleman Casey was a sturdy man in his early 30s, with a calm demeanour and a strong sense of duty that set him apart in the small rural village he patrolled. Standing tall and broad-shouldered, he carried himself with quiet confidence, his clean-shaven face often set in a thoughtful expression. His dark brown hair was neatly combed under the brim of his Royal Irish Constabulary (RIC) helmet, and his steady blue eyes exuded both authority and fairness.

Coleman grew up in a neighbouring village, the son of a blacksmith, and his upbringing instilled in him a strong work ethic and a belief in justice. He joined the constabulary not out of loyalty to the Crown but because he saw it as a way to bring order and protection to his community. He was deeply aware of the tensions simmering in Ireland and treaded a careful line between enforcing the law and maintaining the trust of the people.

Constable Casey is known for his even-handedness, treating everyone with respect regardless of their social standing or political beliefs. While he upheld the law, he was not blindly rigid, he listened to both sides of a dispute and strived to find resolutions that were fair and compassionate. His ability to empathise with the struggles of the villagers made him a figure of quiet respect, even among those who resented British rule.

Coleman was not naive to the complexities of his role; he understood the growing unrest and sympathised with those who sought a better life. However, he believed in maintaining peace above all else and used his position to de-escalate conflicts whenever possible. He was a man of integrity who refused to misuse his authority, even when pressured by his superiors.

Though Constable Casey was sometimes seen as caught between two worlds, the Crown he served and the Irish people he understood, he remained steadfast in his principles. His fair and level-headed approach made him a rare figure of trust in a time of growing uncertainty and division.

It was the year 1913.

Pat and Jimmy had been told the day's chores earlier.

Pat was thinking about Alice, a girl from the nearby townland. They had spent the previous evening together chatting about their hopes for the future and as he left her, he had stolen a kiss.

Jimmy was whistling and in much better mood than usual. Jimmy was 28 and was a casual hand on the farm owned by Pat's father.

Pat's father Pete was a big brute of a man and demonstrated how hard work should be done. There was no tolerance for weakness.

Today Pete was in a ferocious bad mood, his pocket watch wasn't where he had left it and had roared at Kate for carelessly putting it somewhere.

He went to yoke up the horses. He was going to town. The horses were, in his opinion, the life blood of the farm and as such were treated better than any sons, daughters, his wife Kate or any farm hand.

Two of the three horses drew the big cart. The third was a plough horse.

Pat had six brothers and two sisters. The boys had left to escape the brutality of their father.

The oldest girl, Noreen, had been meeting a boy secretly and had left a short letter to her mother explaining that she was leaving and not to worry. The boys saw this as an act of bravery and left weeks later.

Pat and his remaining sister Mol were the only two left.

Their house was one of the biggest in the parish. It had been built recently and still required some drainage works to be completed. It stood on one hundred acres of reasonable to poor land. The condition of the land was due to it being low lying with inadequate drainage.

Kate had notions of grandeur and tried to keep the two-storey house looking like the style of the British landlords' houses. Her parlour contained fancy ornate furniture and a piano, luxurious drapes and rugs.

Nobody but her dared enter this room.

Pat and Jimmy had been picking spuds for the past few days and today were drawing the spuds by cart to a pit in a garden adjacent to the house.

A hole had been dug at the corner of the house by the builder for a soak away rainwater dispersal system. Pat's father had observed him slacking and *ran him out the gate*.

The cart drawing the spuds was pulled up and the two men proceeded to carry them by bucket to the prepared pit.

After a period of time Jimmy stopped and gazed up at the autumn sun.

Pat looked at him. This was indeed unusual behaviour.

Jimmy had a faraway look in his eyes.

Pat was starting to get greatly annoyed. He believed if anyone should be in good spirits it was he.

After all he had a girl. Jimmy had nothing to be cheerful about.

Then Jimmy spoke. He said, "Once I have the passage fare, we will be away from the drudgery of this place."

Pat looked at him bemused.

"Passage?" Pat said.

"The boat to England," Jimmy stated.

"What would take you off there?" Pat asked.

"We are eloping," Jimmy replied.

"We?" said Pat.

"Yes, myself and my lady friend are going off from this place altogether."

Pat was astounded.

"Christ," Pat said, "I never heard you talk about a lady before, is it your sister you'd be going off with?"

Jimmy got irritated with this insinuation and blurted out, "Actually it's Alice Duffy that I'm going with."

Pat looked at him not believing what he was hearing.

"Alice from down the road there? Do ya mean…?" his voice breaking.

"The very one," Jimmy said. "Do you know the family?"

Pat was speechless.

He started trembling with a strange fear, rage maybe. He had an uncontrollable urge to scream.

Jimmy lit a match and put it to his pipe and puffed to get it going.

This irritated Pat more than anything.

"Alice Duffy, you say," he uttered.

Jimmy ignored that statement and proceeded to mimic how he would propose marriage when they reached England. He got down on one knee.

He looked up at Pat as if proposing to him instead.

Pat lifted a spade and struck Jimmy a vicious blow.

He watched as the life went out of Jimmy's body.

In a panic he tumbled the body over and it dropped into the soak-away pit.

He looked about for something to conceal the body with. He ran to the outhouse and looked at the items hung on the walls. Old bridles, harnesses and pull-ups. He grabbed the oilskin pull-ups and went back to the hole. He covered Jimmy and picked random stones from the top of the garden wall hoping the missing stones wouldn't be noticed. Once the body was covered, he picked up the spade again and filled the hole completely. He walked around in a daze for a minute or two. He spotted a barrel under a down-pipe at the back of the house. Quickly he remembered where there was an empty barrel not in use. He fetched it and placed it above where the hole was. This is good, he thought.

Where will I say Jimmy is if my father asks? he thought.

Would it be enough to say I don't know?

Christ, he thought.

Jimmy's bicycle. He ran to the shed and checked that his mother or Mol were not about. He lifted the bicycle on to his shoulder and made his way to the boundary with the neighbouring land. He climbed the fence and again checked that the coast was clear. He crossed the field to a gate leading onto the road.

He carefully set the bicycle against the ditch inside the gate. He knew people often did this as he had done so himself. He believed that anyone concerned would simply think Jimmy met someone, ditched his bicycle and travelled on.

He paced about trembling, fear within him making it difficult to think straight. He climbed over the gate and looked up and down the road. He had to pull himself together. He waited until his breathing was more settled. Then he quickly returned home the way he had come.

❧ ❧ ❧ ❧

Alice watched from the scullery window waiting to see Jimmy coming all evening and when the supper was long over, she returned to the window. Her mother asked her why she didn't make herself useful, but she ignored her.

The baby was growing inside her, she thought. She made numerous excuses for Jimmy being late until she spotted a figure in the distance.

Her heart fluttered with relief. She knew Pete Flaherty was a devil to work for and that he would take his sweet time giving Jimmy his day's pay.

She squinted her eyes at the shape getting closer. That's not Jimmy, she thought. Her heart sank. It was that bloody Pat Flaherty. A pest of a lad that had airs and graces about himself. And the cheeky bugger had tried to kiss her the other evening.

Where was he going? she asked herself. To her horror he turned in the gate and loudly knocked on the door.

Mick Duffy, her father went to the door and greeted Pat, "Well Pat. Anything wrong?"

"I was wanting to see if Alice would care to walk with me for a bit," he said.

Alice was mortified and a bit curious at the same time. Surely, he didn't believe…Could he believe…?

She sprang out past her father and said in passing that she wouldn't be very long.

When they were down road a bit, she asked Pat what was the meaning of his calling. Pat had a giddy aloofness that she hadn't noticed before.

He said, "I know that Jimmy had notions about you and him, but I put him straight. I told him to steer clear as we were walking out."

Alice was stunned into silence.

"Walking out," she eventually uttered. "We are not doing anything of the sort, Pat Flaherty and let that be the end of it."

However, Pat wasn't giving up that easily.

He then said, "Jimmy left today after hearing that you and I had kissed and that you were very agreeable to my advances going forward."

Alice was indignant. "How dare you make such assumptions? Where is Jimmy now?" she asked with a tremor in her voice.

"Jimmy is gone," he said. "He left without speaking to my father."

Alice turned on the road and quickened her step back to the house.

"Leave me alone," she muttered towards Pat.

Alice's father had been at the gate watching them and said to Pat when he tried to keep pace with Alice, "Be off with yourself now Pat, 'tis getting late."

When he got inside, he confronted Alice, their only child.

"You will get yourself a bad reputation, my girl. You cannot be playing one lad against the other.

It will end badly if you keep that up."

Alice looked at him with tears in her eyes. "Everything is so unfair," she blurted.

Alice went to her room, closed the door gently and cried.

She refused to believe Jimmy would ever do this to her.

What now? she thought.

Alice and her parents were regular mass goers, and she would have listened to what was said about hussies having sex before marriage. Mother and baby homes.

The shame her parents would feel. Alice cried harder at the thought.

Her mind went back to Pat.

❧ ❧ ❧ ❧

Pete admired the fine pit of spuds and looked at Pat's handiwork filling in the hole left by the lazy builder. He was astounded at Pat's initiative with the barrel. He didn't see him having such foresight.

He was content that Pat had married even if the girl was a cottager. He would have liked a sizeable dowry to have accompanied her, instead she came with nothing.

Pat wasn't kind to Alice, but Alice didn't seem to care very much.

Kate watched the girl curiously. She wasn't a patch on Mol. Mol was constantly working. The cows were milked, cream separated, butter made, eggs collected, bread baked, pigs fed, and she tended to the vegetable garden that ran down to the road. Kate thought she saw Mol speaking on occasion with the farm hand that worked on the neighbouring farm.

❧ ❧ ❧ ❧

Mol got the chores completed as quickly as possible every day. She then had gotten into the way of weeding and picking the carrots and parsnips that were ready.

The farm hand Joe, from down the way worked for a childless couple. They were kind decent people that kept to themselves.

Mol and Joe chatted at every opportunity. Joe lived alone and was plucking up the courage to speak with Mol's father about walking out with his daughter.

Joe and Mol talked mostly about politics and the goings on up and down the country.

Joe was a quiet man that mostly listened to Mol. Mol was also quiet but seemed to find Joe's company a great ease for her.

And after Sunday mass, Joe tapped Pete on the shoulder.

"I'd like your permission to walk out with your daughter, Mr Flaherty," Joe said.

"Indeed, you can Joe. She's a good woman," Pete said. " 'Tis not ideal having three women in the kitchen," he went on.

࿔ ࿔ ࿔ ࿔

Alice's ears pricked up when she heard Mol's news. Alice was to chaperone.

On the second walk as chaperone, Joe mentioned that Jimmy's bicycle was still where he had first seen it. Alice was crestfallen. She had put all thoughts of Jimmy out of her mind. This was a big revelation as the walks were mostly in silence.

What did this mean? she tried to think.

Jimmy lived with his parents, brother and two sisters in the opposite direction to where Joe had found the bicycle.

The next day Alice took a half dozen eggs and cycled the two miles to Jimmy's home place.

She spoke to a girl a little younger herself in the front garden. "I've brought some eggs," Alice announced. "The hens are laying like mad." Alice introduced herself and stretched out her hand to the girl.

"Where's Jimmy?" the girl asked abruptly.

"I am just leaving you some eggs," Alice said again and because she didn't know what else say.

"Jimmy," Alice then muttered.

"Yes, Jimmy. He hasn't come home in two months. Did you refuse to go with him?" she asked.

"He told me of his plan. He told me he wanted to marry you. Did you turn him down?"

Alice turned the bicycle and rushed away.

❧ ❧ ❧ ❧

Pete was in town. He was a commanding figure on the big cart drawn by two fine brood mares.

He needed meal, flour and a pocket watch. He hadn't found the watch that he blamed his wife Kate for moving. He had spoken very little to her since.

After he had his provisions, he pulled the cart up outside Lynch's public house. He enjoyed the admiration he received when he entered.

The dozen or so men in the bar tipped their hats to Pete. Pete ordered a bottle of stout.

"Begodden we haven't seen Jimmy in ages," Dennis Cusack said.

"He left without so much as a by-your-leave" Pete answered to no one in particular.

On the road home Pete thought about Jimmy. He was due five shillings. Why did he leave without saying a word, without his money? It didn't make any sense, Pete thought.

He lifted his new watch out of his waistcoat pocket and checked the time.

As he passed Jimmy's home he seen his sister in the front garden. She stared at him without acknowledging him. Pete felt a little uneasy.

Alice listened as Pete told of his encounter in Lynch's and the stare from Jimmy's sister. Mol then chipped in with the bicycle being found where it was.

Alice decided to say nothing of her meeting with the sister. It would unravel against her, she thought.

Six months later Alice's son James was born. He came early, she told anyone that she met.

Kate wasn't fooled. She seen that the marriage was without any affection. She barely acknowledged Pat.

Pat had taken to slipping into Lynch's public house in the evenings. He didn't receive the adulation that his father did, however the few bottles of stout eased the anxiety and loneliness he felt. He worried constantly that his crime would be discovered.

"Any word of Jimmy?" he was asked on occasion. "He's in England as far as I know," Pat would reply.

This evening there was a group of strangers in the bar. Pat overheard them mention an uprising. He had heard his father and Mol speak of these things. He lifted his stout and headed off to join the group. His lack of knowledge regarding events in Ireland had the men suspicious that he could be an informer for the British. However, a regular came and sat with them and when asked if he could vouch for this new member he laughed loudly. "Pat couldn't fight his shadow without his father's permission, sure."

He was in.

He hadn't really known what was happening, but he got carried along with the talk of guns and freedom.

He liked the feeling of being wanted and he had already killed after all. He decided it better to keep that to himself.

They arranged to meet again the following evening.

Jimmy's sister Eve stepped into the Royal Irish Constabulary (RIC) station in the town. She asked for Constable Coleman Casey. Eve knew Jimmy and Coleman had been friends in school. He came out to meet her and sensing her nervousness he took her into a holding cell where they could speak.

Eve explained that Jimmy had disappeared without trace from his place of work and needed him to make discreet enquiries. She told of her encounter with Alice and that she was worried about him.

Coleman said he would do his utmost.

Coleman went the next day to the Flaherty farm. Alice opened the door and directed him to the tackle shed where Pete and Pat were both working separately. Pete was filing one of the horses' hooves and Pat was straightening nails on a small anvil.

They both stopped what they were doing when they saw Coleman at the shed entrance.

Coleman introduced himself and said he was making enquiries about the whereabouts of Jimmy White.

Pete recommenced filing the hoof whilst stating that Jimmy left without a bye or leave. Pat, his back to Coleman, had a hammer in his hand but was not using it. Coleman thought it unusual but continued to address Pete.

Pete said Jimmy was a big loss as he had been a good worker.

Coleman bid the men good day without receiving a response.

He hopped on his bicycle and a short distance from the house he was stopped by Alice and her baby James. She told him she had been courting Jimmy and like everybody else was shocked when he just left. She told him about his bicycle being left where it was found and at that they parted ways.

Coleman knew Pat had started to frequent Flynn's pub in town. He wouldn't be able to enter the establishment due to the current unrest, but it would be watched from a distance, he decided.

The following Monday evening Pat asked his father if he could take the big cart to town to collect straw he had been offered. Pete was delighted with his son's enthusiasm and agreed instantly.

Pat drove the big horse drawn cart to town, and it was filled with loose straw.

He then took the cart to the RIC station. He was to get as many of the twelve constabulary outside the station as he possibly could.

He pulled up the horses and engaged the brake on the big cart. He called out for assistance and a Constable appeared. He said, "There is a big row in Lynch's public house, the good local people are fighting against members of the Brotherhood." The Constable stepped away inside the door and relayed what Pat had announced.

A group of Constables bearing rifles quickly assembled outside the station. The Sergeant told Pat to be on his way. Pat released the brake and guns started firing from under the straw.

When the last Constable was shot the men climbed out from beneath the straw and entered the station. They ordered the ammunition store be opened and with the remaining two Constables on the ground they loaded the cart with their bounty. On leaving, the two remaining men were shot dead.

Pat felt elated that he had played such a pivotal role in the operation. They were to lie low for a time until the backlash they expected calmed down.

The RIC were out in force. Coleman hadn't been on duty and was summoned to give as much insight as he could about the men that could possibly have been involved. The only evidence left was hoof marks, cart tracks and straw on the ground.

Pete heard about what happened the next day but never connected his son with the atrocity.

Mol noticed Pat's nervous expression but didn't make any comment.

Alice cared less about Pat. Whenever she received any advance from him she feigned illness to avoid interacting.

Kate noticed this and avoided any conversation with Alice.

Coleman sat with his Sergeant and spoke about the comings and goings in the neighbourhood around the town. The one thing of note was the disappearance of Jimmy White. "He just vanished," Coleman stated. "Nobody just vanishes," the Sergeant said.

"Could he be one of the Brotherhood?" he asked Coleman in a way that implied, 'have you thought of that possibility.'

That threw Coleman. He hadn't even considered that.

"That would make sense right enough," Coleman said, his mind working on overdrive to piece it together.

The bicycle could have been a decoy.

Stay out of contact with family so not to endanger them.

Pat Flaherty must know something.

"Arrest him," the Sergeant said.

"Go armed and bring two Constables along with you."

Pat had found what was missing in his life. He felt alive having been part of something so extraordinary.

He cared not a bit about the men that had lost their lives. They were British agents, he said to himself.

They had it coming. He wanted more. He would wait to be summoned to the next meeting. Soon he hoped.

The dog growled from under the table in the kitchen. There was a loud knock on the door.

Alice opened the door and was shocked to see Eve standing there.

"I want to know where Jimmy is," she half shouted at Alice.

Pete looked at the girl in the doorway.

Before he got a chance to speak the dog barked and the sight of a group of RIC men in uniform caused Alice to stand back into the kitchen followed by Eve.

"We demand to know the whereabouts of Jimmy White," Coleman said loudly.

Pete stood up with his big frame making him a formidable presence.

One of the Constables raised his rifle. "Don't move," the Constable said.

The dog sensing the aggression coming from the Constable sprang out from below the table and attacked the Constable's ankles. Pete called the dog off and he retreated to beneath the table.

Pat spoke, "Jimmy is gone from here. He went off to England. He left us shorthanded."

Eve said, "Jimmy would've told me if he was doing that. Jimmy is a good man, a kind man. You know that don't you, Alice?" she continued whilst looking directly at Alice.

Alice was lost for words.

"How would she know?" Kate said. Everyone turned to look at Kate. She rarely spoke anymore and to hear her speak was a surprise and more so what she had asked.

"She and Jimmy were planning to make a life together," Eve said.

Everyone's gaze now turned on Pat.

Mol was in the vegetable garden chatting to Joe and watching the events up at the house.

She decided it best to get a first-hand look into what was going on. She walked up the garden with a bunch of carrots in her hand. She excused herself and entered the kitchen. She set the carrots onto the table and looked about all the faces.

"Would you people care for a cup of tea?" she asked in the direction of the RIC officers.

"We are on official business, mam," Coleman said. "We are asking if Jimmy White has been in contact."

Mol was surprised that Jimmy's whereabouts was a concern after the recent events.

"Pat Flaherty, you are coming with us," Coleman said.

Pete was shocked and asked, "What it has to do with my son?"

"That's what we intend to find out," Coleman said.

"I knew you had something to with it," Eve said. "You and her," pointing at Alice.

Mol was thinking hard.

Pat was in the holding cell when the Sergeant and Coleman entered. Pat hadn't had enough time to get his story straight when they entered. However, he had a massive stroke of luck. The Sergeant slipped up with his opening line of questioning.

He asked Pat if Jimmy was involved with the Brotherhood. Pat was told no harm would come to him if he told them the truth from the outset.

Pat thought for a few seconds. This could work out well if he answered correctly.

"Do you know…?" Pat started. "I had a feeling that he could be. He had been acting strange in the while before he left that day. All I know is that he said something about a passage fare and to be truthful, I didn't know what he was talking about. I have gone into Lynch's a few times asking was there any sign of him, but nobody tells me anything."

"Are there some strangers going into Flynn's that you could tell us about?" Coleman asked.

Again, Pat thought if he could act innocently, he might pull this off.

"There are a group of lads," Pat said. "They are *smart aleck's*," he continued.

"They are picking late spuds up at the big house, they say."

"Who says that, Pat?" Coleman asked.

"Dennis Cusack said it to me," Pat replied.

Coleman looked at the Sergeant and nodded. The Sergeant looked back at Pat and studied him for a moment.

"Go home," he said to Pat.

Pat left and before leaving town he slipped into Flynn's.

Dennis Cusack was there.

Coleman and his Sergeant sat in the holding room.

"There was a similar ambush in Passage West in Limerick recently," the Sergeant said to Coleman. "Could that be what Jimmy was saying?"

Coleman thought about this and found it hard to fathom that a thick like Jimmy could be involved in such organised raids.

He remembered Jimmy to be a simple thick young lad.

No ambition. But maybe that was the sort of them insurgents.

Coleman watched Dennis Cusack leave Flynn's and stepped quickly to match his stride. He guided Dennis down the alley beside the RIC station.

"Tell me Mr Cusack, what business has them strange lads in Flynn's?"

"What?" shouted Dennis. "I'm not answering your questions." "Answer me," Coleman said aggressively "or I'll give you what's for."

"Sure, they are picking late spuds up at the big house," Dennis said with a smirk on his face.

Coleman was downbeat. A little wary of the word-perfect collaboration with what Pat had said.

At Sunday Mass the whereabouts of the Brotherhood meeting was circulated. Tuesday evening at nine. Travel to the safe house was to be discreet with attendees making certain they were not followed.

A large group of twenty-two men had gathered. There was quiet muttering amongst the men. Pat knew the main man was coming and there was anticipated hope he would be singled out for praise. He was surprised to see Joe, the man that was seeing Mol, there.

"Shush," was uttered quietly.

Mol entered the room.

She looked around.

"Comrádaithe

ná bad le duine ar bith, táimid ag cogadh.

ní bheidh sos againn go dtí go mbeidh ár n-Éire ionúin athghairmthe
againn.

Bíodh fear ar bith nach bhfuil sásta troid agus bás a fháil ar ár gcúis
chóir, fág anois."

She addressed the room in native Irish tongue.

"Comrades

Let no man be fooled, we are at war.

We will not rest until we have reclaimed our beloved Ireland.

Let any man not prepared to fight and die for our just cause, leave now."

Pat was horrified beyond belief.

His sister that was a simple girl. How could this be?

He wanted to tell her to be a good girl and go home to her chickens.

But instead, he said nothing and listened to her and begrudgingly admired the respect she had of the men.

RIC interrogation methods were discussed through a mock interrogation setup.

One man was sat on a chair, blindfolded and questioned. Each answer was discussed, each mistake corrected and still Pat sat motionless.

❧ ❧ ❧ ❧

After Eve's visit to the house, Alice had walked her home. They agreed to meet again and today was the day.

Alice decided to trust Eve and tell her what had happened. She had kept the trauma of the whole situation to herself.

Eve questioning Jimmy's absence made Alice feel less abandoned.

She told Eve about her pregnancy and that she was an aunt to James.

Eve immediately took the child from Alice and looked at him. "Jesus, he's the spit of Jimmy," she said. "Why the Christ didn't you say?"

Alice recalled her days of the most terrifying anxiety when Pat said Jimmy had left.

Eve now understood that Alice was in the same quandary as herself and she felt a warm connection towards her.

❧ ❧ ❧ ❧

Mol was alone in her thoughts.

She had considered letting her brother Pat fall on his face from the outset.

She had watched Jimmy and Pat at the spuds and seen Pat strike Jimmy. When she saw Jimmy being rolled over into the hole she ran to the end of the garden and waved her arms until Joe spotted her and came to their spot.

Joe had crossed the road into the garden and together they had watched Pat.

Mol decided after watching the barrel being set in place that this could jeopardise the whole operation.

They watched Pat lift the bicycle and take off across the field. That was when she set the plan.

Joe ran and moved the barrel; he dug out the loose soil and set the stones at one side. He lifted the body out and carried it to the bottom of the garden. He ran back, filled the hole and replaced the barrel. He stood back and noticed his footprints. He got on his knees and brushed soil over the prints with his hands. He ran to the bottom of the garden. He was about to put the body over his shoulder when he stopped, did he just see movement?

Mol appeared at Joe's shoulder.

"Mol, I think he is alive," Joe said.

"No time for that now," Mol said with urgency in her tone. "Get him across the road, he is on his way back. Fetch the cart. Put hay or have ye straw over there? Put it in the cart to cover him. If he is alive take him to your house and I will arrange the rest."

Mol's thoughts now were congested. They needed more men, more guns, more ammunition and better communication. She noticed the RIC were focusing on ordinary folk. Looking for change, looking for weakness, looking for anything that could lead them to members of the Brotherhood.

Pat was a liability she had felt, yet he managed to ward off his involvement in the shootings and subsequent arms robbery.

She would think about that later.

❧ ❧ ❧ ❧

Jimmy had been receiving daily visits and care from Mol. She had initially brought a doctor with connections to the Brotherhood, and he had given him a slim chance of survival due to potential spinal damage and subsequent brain damage.

Jimmy sat up on his own yesterday. Mol wasn't sure what she should do or say to him.

She thought about Alice. She thought about Eve. She thought about Pat, her father and her mother. What a bloody mess!

❧ ❧ ❧ ❧

Connolly, their leader was planning a visit due to the recent successes to explain and outline the intensification of the attacks against the British. She wanted to impress upon him that her unit was tight and ready for new instruction. Mol needed to remove one or both of the antagonists to ensure the safety of the Brotherhood.

❧ ❧ ❧ ❧

Jimmy was sore. He remembered little about what had happened. He remembered Pat's twisted look before he felt the blow.

Now he was ready to find himself and get his life back.

❧ ❧ ❧ ❧

Mol decided to take Eve to see Jimmy.

She thought if she put Alice's situation to him, he might understand.

❧ ❧ ❧ ❧

Pat was restless. He had no interest in the chores his father kept giving him. He wanted the adrenaline rush of being involved in tasks for the Brotherhood. Connolly was coming to talk to them. He would get recognition he thought.

Pete noticed that Pat was uninterested in the farm. He felt demoralised. His wife didn't speak to him or anyone else for that matter.

He decided to go to town. A couple of bottles of stout would give him some solace he thought.

❧ ❧ ❧ ❧

Pete entered Flynn's public house.

He didn't receive the usual adulation, he felt.

"A bottle of stout," he asked of Tom the bar tender.

He stood alone in silence.

Strange indeed, he thought.

❧ ❧ ❧ ❧

Mol called at Eve's home.

Eve had watched her approach and met her at the door.

"Will you come for a walk?" Mol requested.

Eve pulled the door closed and walked alongside Mol.

They talked about everything except Jimmy. Eve wanted to ask. Mol wanted to say.

Instead, they talked about Mol and Joe's romance and the events around the country.

The attacks against the British had increased and their popularity was growing considerably.

Mol was surprised with how much knowledge Eve had and her passion for the success of the Brotherhood.

They arrived at the house and were greeted by Joe. Eve entered the room where Jimmy was sitting on a chair. She felt weak, unable to speak, her hands shaking, her body was shaking. She was unable to speak.

❧ ❧ ❧ ❧

Alice sat with James. Her only joy.

Eve was a joy, but she couldn't fill the void. She had little money but could scrape enough to get the boat to England. She had an aunt there that had visited once. She was a pleasant woman and Alice thought she would get her a position in a big house possibly.

Alice counted her money and decided she would leave rather than suffer the silence and pain here.

She would leave first thing in the morning.

෭ ෭ ෭ ෭

Jimmy had big tears in his eyes.

He would kill Pat Flaherty, was his immediate reaction.

He hated Alice, was another.

He had a son, that brought the tears.

Eve explained the sacrifice Alice had made.

He didn't see it as sacrifice as she had married that brute so soon.

Eve calmed him down and explained again that Pat had said, "You were gone. What was the girl to do?"

෭ ෭ ෭ ෭

Kate heard Alice being up early and made an effort to avoid her. As Alice rushed to get away she caught a glimpse of her bag. She turned to face her.

"Where are you off to?" she asked.

Alice hadn't a prepared answer as she didn't expect any notice to be taken of her.

"I'm going to…" she paused. "I'm going to town," she blurted out.

Kate sensed that there was more to this journey.

"What will you do when you get to where you are going?" she asked.

Tears welled up in Alice's eyes.

Nobody had taken a bit of notice of her in all the time she lived in this house.

"I can't bear it anymore," she said in a quiet voice.

"Women like us have to make do with our lot," Kate said. "We don't get to choose. Don't you realise you will be a cast out wherever you go? Think about your child, what will become of that little mite?"

Alice gathered her thoughts.

Had she thought this through? Who would look after James if she managed to secure a position? She turned around and decided to rethink it all and decide later.

She quietly made her way back to the bedroom. She was setting the bag down when he started the beating.

He hadn't laid a hand on her in weeks but this morning he was angry. He must have been listening and heard what his mother had said to her.

Why else would he be angry?

Mol heard the commotion between Pat and Alice.

He would kill the poor girl, she thought.

What was she to do? Mind my own business, she considered. Sending him on a Brotherhood mission would be sending him to his death. She decided to involve her father.

Pete and Mol worked side by side placing loose stones on top of a crumbling wall. Animals frequently scratched themselves against the jagged stones for comfort.

Mol decided that now was the time.

"Pat was no interest in farming, has he?"

"It is a pity."

Then she kept quiet.

"I have been thinking about little else," he said after a time. "I will pay his fare to America, over to his brother Connor."

Mol hadn't expected this.

"What about Alice and the child?" Mol asked.

"Do you know…" he started, "they are not a match? She has no time for him nor he her, no time for the young ladeen either. He might take up the offer quicker if he was to go on his own."

Mol couldn't believe the wisdom of her father.

But he wasn't finished yet.

"You and Joe are tight," he said. "Are ye for tying the knot? You can stay where you are, and sure Joe can join you. He could come and work the farm with me. Sure, it would be yours when we're gone."

Mol tried to take all this in.

The problems she had now included:

Would Pat accept?

Would Alice agree?

Would Jimmy agree?

What would she do with Jimmy? He was a wanted man even though he had done nothing wrong.

Would Jimmy want to be with Alice?

Would Alice want Jimmy?

How or where would they live?

& & & &

Kate spoke to Pete in the tackle shed.

"What are we to do with them two?" she opened with. "They despise each other."

Pat sat on a stool and took his pipe from his pocket.

He cut off thin slithers of tobacco from a block into his open hand, he rubbed the tobacco into his palm with the base of his other hand, then turned the pipe sideways and pushed the tobacco into its chamber. The he struck a match and puffed. "Ahhh," he said, "we will send him over to Connor, he has no interest in the farm."

Kate looked at him, disbelieving. "And let Mol in here with Joe, I suppose. What about the girl and her child then?"

"That will sort itself without us interfering," said Pete.

"It's settled then," Kate said.

"Aye," said Pete.

& & & &

Alice and Mol sat in the kitchen. Alice was thinking if Jimmy could have been involved in any way.

She needed to know the extent of trouble he was suspected to be involved in. It had to be just conjecture. But the RIC were sore. They could pin it on him without a question being asked. Jimmy was in danger without a doubt.

Mol spoke first. "I know where Jimmy is."

Alice stopped and stared at her. "What do you mean?"

Mol tried to read her reaction to the news. "He had been in an altercation with your husband. He got seriously hurt and was taken away to be cared for. It was only when he recently managed to regain his speech that his association with you became known."

Alice tried to understand what Mol was telling her.

Jimmy was here. He hadn't abandoned her after all.

"I want to see him," she said.

"Yes of course, Alice. I'm sure you do. But just one thing. Jimmy being missing was noticed by the RIC. They are looking for him in connection with the murders at the station and the stolen ammunition. Jimmy had nothing to do with that, but he is in the frame for it. They will be most likely watching your movements hoping you will lead them to Jimmy."

❧ ❧ ❧ ❧

Jimmy was afraid to move. He wanted more than anything to see Alice and his son. Why did this happen? he asked himself.

He thought about his options.

Sail from Cobh in County Cork, he had never been that far. Belfast could be a safer route but from the West of Ireland, it was a long journey. How could he get Alice to agree to go with him now? Eve could deliver a message to her. Feel her out to see if she was agreeable.

He had some money but scarcely enough. What life could he offer her and his son? He cursed Pat Flaherty.

❧ ❧ ❧ ❧

Mol instructed Alice to visit the RIC station and seek out Constable Coleman Casey.

She proceeded to the station and waited to see Coleman. She recalled their last conversation.

Coleman was cold towards her when he appeared.

"Have you heard anything of Jimmy?" she asked.

"Jimmy is a wanted man," he replied with venom in his tone.

"How can that be?" she exclaimed. "He wouldn't hurt a fly. You remember Jimmy. Always kind. What makes you think he could commit a crime?"

"He disappeared when or just before certain atrocities were committed. He had mentioned one of the places to your husband, Alice," he said.

"That's impossible," she responded. "Jimmy just wouldn't."

"Have you heard of or seen him?" he asked.

"Nobody has," she replied and left.

That confirms what Mol said. Jimmy is in the frame, she surmised.

∾ ∾ ∾ ∾

"You can go off over to Connor," Pete said to Pat.

Pat turned to face his father and asked him to repeat what he had said. "You heard me the first time. The boat leaves Cobh two weeks tomorrow. I will pay the passage for you and Connor will set you to find employment."

Rage filled Pat's head again. The same rage that had him kill that Jimmy lad.

"I'll do no such a thing. I have a wife and a child and this place to run. Why would I want to go off there?"

"Two weeks tomorrow from Cobh," Pete repeated.

"Gather a few things and bring a letter to Connor," from his mother, inside.

Pat's rage simmered. His mother knew about this madness too.

This cannot be happening, he raged. He had found his happy place at last, and he thought they were going to take it away from him.

Pete watched his son. His eyes darting around the tack shed. He seen his eyes rest on a metal spike. What was he thinking? Pete wondered.

"You are not suited to Alice," Pete resumed speaking with a calm tone. "That child is not your son."

Pat's rage boiled over. He reached for the metal spike and raised it, ready to strike his father.

"Stop," Mol said in the commanding tone she had used at the meeting. "Go from here now."

Pat stopped but didn't know why he had. What control did she have over him? Yet he understood and obeyed her order.

Mol moved closer to her father.

Ba rud maith é a tháinig nuair a rinne mé athair.

tá stríoc contúirteach sa chomhluadar sin.

"It was a good thing I came when I did father. There is a dangerous streak in that lad."

❧ ❧ ❧ ❧

Eve travelled carefully on Mol's advice to see Jimmy.

She picked wildflowers from hedges as she walked, to give her opportunity to look around for any sign that she was being followed.

Jimmy was delighted to have a visitor as he rarely saw anyone except Mol.

Eve agreed to take a letter to Alice.

Mo Ghrá

Is oth liom an méid a tharla. Tuigim go raibh ort an cinneadh a rinne tú a dhéanamh.

Fanann mo mhothúcháin ar do shon gan athrú. Tá súil agam go mbraitheann tú mar an gcéanna.

Is mise i gcónaí.

My Love

I regret so much what happened. I understand that you had to make the decision you did.

My feelings for you remain unchanged. I do hope you feel the same.

Yours always.

The letter was short, in native tongue and unsigned for fear of discovery.

Alice held the letter to her chest and cried for hours.

She cursed Pat Flaherty.

❧ ❧ ❧ ❧

Pat went to Lynch's.

He asked for a bottle of stout.

He got no response. He asked again.

"You are not getting a drink, Pat," the bar owner said. "Leave quietly now, there's a good man."

Everyone is gone mad around here, he muttered to himself.

He felt alone now.

❧ ❧ ❧ ❧

Mol made an extra bed up in her small room. She took it and gave hers to Alice and James. She decided Alice wouldn't get another hand laid on her by her brute of a brother.

Pat bedded down in the tack room. He was sulking. He felt sure they would withdraw their standoffish stance they had adopted towards him.

He needn't have bothered he thought; nobody took any notice.

In the morning, he was in a rage. He was hungry and he would have to go into the kitchen to get something to eat.

When he entered, no one spoke to him.

He pushed Alice off the chair she was sitting on and said, "Get out of my way, you filthy hure."

Mol took Alice by the arm into the parlour. Alice had never set foot in this room before now.

Mol returned to the kitchen.

"You will leave for Cobh tomorrow," she started.

"Indeed, I won't," he uttered.

"The rainwater is not getting away from the corner of the house," she said looking toward her father.

Pat looked up startled.

"Cobh, tomorrow," she said.

❧ ❧ ❧ ❧

Alice looked around the room. It was beautiful. Its clean walls, the stunning drapes and stylish furniture. It all worked so well. She suddenly felt admiration for Kate. This was her life. This was her haven. She turned suddenly. Kate was sitting silently in a chair. "I'm sorry, I shouldn't be in here."

"Sit down please," Kate said. "I can see that you like the room as I do."

"He is of my blood," she started. "But there is an ugly streak in him. He is being sent away to America because no good will become of him here. You and your child's safety made up part of that decision making. Mol told me what happened with Jimmy. The poor lad didn't deserve that, and I can see the predicament that left you in."

Pat decided he had no choice but to go. He wouldn't ever come back. He would show them. He had little money, he thought, but he did have a valuable item. He grinned. He stuffed his little possessions into a bag and went to the tack room. Fear set in as soon as he looked up.

He rushed to the spot where he had left it. He had taken it and hidden it in the oilskins that were hanging there. You are a stupid, stupid gombeen, he said.

He had covered Jimmy with the oilskins when he was in the panic.

હ હ હ હ

Pete's mother had taken him to Dublin for company when he was only 12 years old. It was such an adventure for the both of them. His mother, May, had some grown-up business with a sister that didn't interest Pete. He busied himself taking in all the sights that were presented.

They stepped off the carriage onto a bustling thoroughfare. So many people in one place. As they walked, he could see people like them and better dressed people with lovely clean clothing. Hats seemed to show people's position in society. Some even had feathers sticking up out of them.

The trams fascinated Pete. So many people being carried along. They boarded a tram to Pete's delight. They sat down and Pete admired the grandeur around him. A gentleman sat opposite smiled at Pete and spoke in a language he never heard before. He attempted to speak in English, but his words were few. Pete wondered what it would be like if his own father looked and dressed like that. He wondered what his father would say to this man. They could speak about the weather I suppose, he thought.

The gentleman stood up and reached out for a hang down grip to steady himself. He had a fancy shirt, a waistcoat, a jacket, a loose scarf and a coat over his arm, in his free hand he held an ornate walking stick. When the tram came to a halt he nodded at Pete and said something that Pete didn't understand. He walked to the opening and stepped off.

Pete saw the beautiful leather bag beneath where he had been sitting. He darted forward and lifted it and rushed to the door. He was jolted back and forth as the tram moved forward. He saw the man look after the tram and then he was out of sight.

Pete went back to his mother and sat down. People were looking at them, him in particular. They got off at the next stop and Pete told his mother to find a place to sit and he started running without waiting for her reply.

He found the man surprisingly quickly and handed him the bag.

"Merci mon garçon, où est ta mère

emmène-moi vers elle."

Thank you, my boy, but where is your mother? Take me to her, he thought he understood based on the man's gestures.

His mother was relieved and happy to see he had helped the gentleman.

"Patek Philippe is my name, madam," he said. "Your boy is good. I have all my work in this bag." He lifted the bag to show her.

"I want to go for tea, would you and the boy…?" he looked at Pete placed a hand on his shoulder and asked, "What is your name, boy?"

"Pete," he uttered.

"Then we shall go for tea, Pete with your mother."

They walked a short distance and turned onto High Street near Christchurch Cathedral, there they entered the Lyons Tea Rooms. Pete never seen such a place and was totally entranced. 'Patrick' as Pete thought he said his name was, watched Pete and took delight in his innocence.

Tea was delivered to their table followed by a hay cock of buns. Pete had never tasted the like of them. The delicate China cups made the experience the greatest day of his life.

Patek sat easily in their company and Pete thought it unusual that a person of his standing would give time to people like us. However, he knew he had done a kind thing running back with his bag. He could have left it where it was.

When they finished their tea Patek wrote on a sheet of beautiful paper his address in a place called Geneva. He tried to explain he came from Poland, but Pete and his mother looked at him absently.

When they stood up Patek took Pete's hand and shook it warmly. "Thank you again, my boy. I want to give you something that you must look after and give it to your son."

He opened the bag and handed Pete a box.

"Look after it well."

On the journey home Pete waited until it was just him and his mother before he withdrew the box from his pocket.

It was made so perfectly. Its gilded edges were a marvel. A small clasp kept the lid secure. His excitement was immense. He undid the clasp and opened the lid. A dark blue velvet piece of material with gold looking thread was revealed. He pulled it to discover it was a pouch. He took it out of its box. It was heavy. Inside he discovered was a gold pocket watch.

It was the most beautiful thing he had ever seen. His mother was amazed at its beauty. He couldn't wait to show his father.

"I will need a waistcoat, mammy," he said.

ﻉ ﻉ ﻉ ﻉ

Pat waited until it was dark. He slowly tipped over the barrel emptying the water. He set it aside.

He dug the soft soil easily until he felt the spade hit a stone. He stepped into the hole and pulled the remaining soil back to one end. What is happening? he thought.

It's not possible. Where the hell is he? He grabbed the spade and attempted to dig deeper. No, he cried. It wasn't that deep. Think man. The oilskins, where are they?

He got up out of the hole and walked about to help him think. He went back to the hole again. He dug until there was nothing left. Not a trace of Jimmy's body. It's not possible, he thought.

ﻉ ﻉ ﻉ ﻉ

When Joe had been summoned by Mol to get Jimmy's body away from the house he had cleared the soil and lifted the oilskins off. As he set them on the bank the watch had fallen out. Joe put it in his pocket and gave it to Mol later that day.

Mol had placed it in its box in the parlour.

She spoke to no one about it.

❧ ❧ ❧ ❧

Kate and Alice were in the parlour with James. They had developed an unlikely friendship that seemed to be born out of respect for each other.

Alice wanted to know how she and Pete had met. Kate told her it was a tough time soon after the famine. Everyone had lost loved ones through starvation or emigration. Nothing was won or gained without hard work. Ensuring survival seemed to be everyone's goal and the work was back-breaking.

It was a mistake to believe you were getting ahead because there would always be a tax to be paid or a relative that was struggling to survive. So, the back-breaking work was relentless.

If a suitor came about the place, they had to have a survival plan of sorts. They were means tested, you might say.

Pete was a hard worker, and everybody knew that. But he also had a kindness which made him popular.

"People like us that had any land acreage worth talking about, had poor wet land. It was tough to get crops out of such wet ground. If it only stopped raining and gave the ground a chance to dry out, you would be able to get by."

The two ladies talked for hours every day.

"After we married," she told Alice, Pete took her on the trip of a lifetime.

"Pete's mother paid for it. We travelled to Geneva. We got the boat in Dublin across to Liverpool. Then we went by stagecoach to Dover, across to France and again stagecoach to Geneva. It was the most amazing journey. Pete remembered a gentleman he and his mother had met in Dublin, and he had his address. We met him and his wife. He took us to the place where he and some other men made the most amazing timepieces. He had given one of them to Pete when he was only a lad.

45

Pete discovered it was worth more money than this farm three times over. Can you believe that?"

Alice loved the story and saw the twinkle in Kate's eyes recalling the time they had.

"He kept the box it came in, you know."

Kate went to the chiffonier and opened the drawer. Behind the drawer there was a hidden compartment. She retrieved the box. She seemed surprised.

Kate opened the box and became delirious with joy. "It's here," she said.

She went quickly to the door and called, "Pete, Pete, Pete come here this instant."

Kate backed into the room and Pete appeared at the door. He looked at Kate and his eyes went to the open box in her outstretched hands.

Pete took out the box. He looked at the box in his hand before removing the velvet pouch. A beaming smile appeared across his big face. Then he looked at Kate.

"The man asked me to look after it and to give it to my son," he said.

Kate loved this big-hearted man.

❧ ❧ ❧ ❧

Mol cycled into town, she was meticulous about routine.

A letter awaited her, and she settled down to discover its contents.

"We are now in the year 1914," it stated,

"Our country, Ireland is a deeply divided society, and different groups have conflicting goals regarding Ireland's political future.

Here's hoping this letter finds you safely.

We outline a summary of what each section of our current society wants.

This, Mol, will help you explain in simple terms to our brothers in arms.

The British Government.

The British government, is led by Prime Minister H.H. Asquith, he wants to implement Home Rule for Ireland through a bill called the Government of Ireland 1914. This legislation would grant Ireland its own parliament with limited powers, while still keeping Ireland as part of the United Kingdom.

Unionists in the north (led by Edward Carson) are fiercely opposed to this Home Rule, fearing it will undermine Protestant dominance and tie them to a Nationalist-majority Ireland.

To address this, the British government are considering the possibility of excluding Ulster (the northern counties) from Home Rule, either temporarily or permanently.

The Irish Volunteers

The Irish Volunteers, as you will know Mol, were formed in 1913 to counter the Ulster Volunteer Force (UVF), which opposed Home Rule.

They want:

Home Rule implemented in full, without the exclusion of Ulster. Many Irish Volunteers are willing to take up arms to defend Ireland's right to self-governance under Home Rule.

The Irish Republican Brotherhood.

We are a secret revolutionary organisation dedicated to the complete independence of Ireland.

We want:

The establishment of an Irish Republic, free from British rule. We reject any form of compromise that keeps Ireland within the United Kingdom.

We now begin planning an armed uprising to achieve independence.

The recent outbreak of The Great War in August 1914 has postponed the implementation of Home Rule, as the British government are focused on the war effort."

Mol was delirious.

❧ ❧ ❧ ❧

Pat felt cornered. No matter what direction he tried to go there was only one open to him. Cobh.

How did it come to this?

He felt part of the movement against the British. He wanted to shout from the treetops that he played a big part in the recent success. He didn't receive the recognition he felt he deserved however, if he was to tell, the real organisers, the men, not Mol, after all what did a woman know about these things? He could dethrone her, the thought formed in his mind.

He stopped himself thinking and realised that he knew nobody in the organisation except Joe and Mol.

❧ ❧ ❧ ❧

Jimmy sat with Mol and Joe.

They were discussing how Jimmy could escape the danger he was in. He understood now that his situation was precarious. They would put him in front of a firing squad to make an example of him.

Alice had written a letter and was so thrilled that he was ok.

Listen to Mol, Alice advised him. They would be together soon enough.

Mol spoke of her proud father and mother. They wouldn't take kindly to an accusation of attempted murder.

"Well, that's what it was!" Jimmy exclaimed.

Joe never interrupted or spoke without a nod from Mol. If she wanted his opinion she would indicate by a nod of her head.

Now Mol nodded towards him.

Joe said, "Act like it never happened at all. Pete Flaherty is a hard but fair man. If the lad goes off as he is supposed to the place will be more at peace. Mind you I'd like to see him walk up the gangway and see the boat off first."

Pat stood near Joe's house and watched the three people with disbelief.

I must be going mad. How could this be? His rage was bubbling again.

He wasn't going to fail once more. This situation presented an opportunity to take Mol's place as head of the unit.

He crept around to the small turf shed, found a length of wood. He tied twine around the middle and brought it to the door. He quietly tied the end of the twine to the door handle. If they tried to open it, they wouldn't be able to.

He crept around the back and lit the thatch in three places. He then lit the front, careful to stay out of sight. He went back to his watch position and delighted in his cleverness.

It was Jimmy who noticed the smell.

"Christ almighty!" said Joe.

"What time is it?" Mol said as she pulled on the door. "It is ten after nine," Joe answered.

"Some of them usually come early."

Two brothers Denny and Kieran Moran saw the flames as they approached. Denny the older started to run towards the house but Kieran held out his hand and stopped him. The two crouched down and moved a bit closer.

"Look," Kieran said.

"See the head."

Denny looked where Kieran's finger was pointing and spotted it.

"Here's what we will do," Kieran whispered.

Denny followed the instructions and started casually walking towards the house to take the lad's attention. Kieran crept up behind him and got him in a headlock. Pat struggled and flicked his head back to try and head butt him backwards, but the grip was tight. He kicked his legs, but he was struggling for breath. He attempted to reach his hands back to grab his assailant, but he couldn't take air into his lungs, he went limp.

Denny released the door and said to Mol, "The coast is clear." They fetched buckets of water and doused the flames but to no avail. The thick straw had taken hold and within seconds it was an inferno.

The remaining men arrived and were told to disperse to the alternative meeting house some distance away.

"Bring him," Mol said, indicating her brother Pat.

"Tie his wrists and ankles, gag and blindfold him," she ordered.

Joe stayed with the burning house while Mol, Jimmy and the others went to the secret location.

Three men were ordered to stay outside and watch for any suspicious movement.

Pat was dumped in a back-room whilst the meeting was commenced.

A gcomrádaithe, táimid ar imeall ár gcuid ama.

Táimid ag druidim lenár gcuid ama.

Tá cumarsáid faighte againn ón oifigeach ceannais, Connolly féin.

Gheobhaidh muid ár neamhspleáchas ceart.

Comrades, we are at the precipice of our time.

We are nearing our time.

We have received communication from our commanding officer, Connolly himself.

We will gain our rightful independence.

"We now must deal with a thorn in our boot.

Denny and Kieran, you both showed your value tonight. We commend you."

All of the men nodded appreciatively in their direction.

"I need two volunteers to escort this individual to Cobh and see him onto the ship sailing for America.

He has the fare on his person so he cannot use that as an excuse not to board the ship. I have a letter you must give to a steward on the ship. His name will be on the envelope. He will keep watch over him for the duration of the passage and our brothers in America will meet him the other side."

Kieran and his brother volunteered.

ܐ ܐ ܐ ܐ

Mol, Jimmy and her father were in the kitchen discussing the fact that the Church was after condemning the The Great War. This action was contributing to a decline in the recruitment of Irish men to the British Army.

Jimmy wasn't terribly interested in politics, but he wanted to be involved in these discussions. He was a great listener, he had been told.

Mol had explained in as little detail as possible to her father around what happened between Pat and Jimmy.

She did say that it was no fault of Jimmy's.

Pete had nodded to this statement.

Mol surprised Pete, she was one of the most articulate girls he ever had encountered. When she had entered the tack shed that day and commanded Pat to stop, Pete had looked at his daughter differently. He admired her like he hadn't really noticed her before. Now she seemed to be the centre of the universe. He loved her aura.

ܐ ܐ ܐ ܐ

Pete and Jimmy were attending the stone mason that was building a small house for Alice and James. It wasn't openly said by anyone that Jimmy and Alice were together but they stole moments together.

James adored his daddy. And talked consistently about him.

Mol was teaching him his Irish but he sometimes got mixed up which everyone laughed at.

Jimmy had to keep a low profile because he wasn't in the clear with the RIC by any means.

Alice needed to get a divorce so that she and Jimmy could be together with their son.

The parish priest wouldn't hear of it.

She wanted to tell him her son wasn't her husband's child but the more she thought about it the more she believed she could get into bigger trouble.

She read the bible to see if there was a way out of her predicament, but it made no reference to such things.

When she talked to Eve she laughed. Eve said she would castrate the bastard, meaning the parish priest.

Alice told her to stop the blasphemy, or they would surely go to hell.

She made an appointment and visited a professional in Galway City.

He informed Alice that obtaining a divorce was extremely rare and legally challenging due to the strong influence of the Church and restrictive divorce laws.

"However, maybe you are a Protestant." "Why?" Alice asked.

"Well, for those who are Protestant, claiming that your marriage was not consummated could be a valid ground for annulment rather than divorce. Here's how you might proceed in such a situation Alice. Non-consummation of marriage is one of the recognised grounds for annulment under British law, which governs Ireland at this time.

"Annulment differs from divorce in that it declares the marriage null and void as if it had never legally existed. Non-consummation is often linked to issues like impotence (the inability of your husband Alice to consummate the marriage), which must be proven in court.

"Alice, if you are a Protestant, you would need to file a case in the Matrimonial Causes Court. As a rule, annulments are typically handled by the Church, but non-consummation is rarely accepted as a ground.

"You would have to provide evidence or testimony to prove that the marriage had never been consummated. In many cases, medical examinations of the husband are ordered to confirm whether he was incapable of consummation (due to impotence or other physical reasons). This process is invasive, requiring detailed testimonies about private marital matters, which will be humiliating for you.

"You will need witnesses or corroborating evidence, which could be difficult to obtain given the private nature of the claim. The courts, Alice, are often biased against women, and proving non-consummation could lead to intense scrutiny.

"I will tell you simply, Alice, the Church, is opposed to both divorce and annulment in most cases. Further they might refuse to recognise the annulment, particularly because you are ."

Alice thought about what she had done marrying Pat. She was in trouble as a Catholic, now what could she do?

As it stands, I am an abandoned mother. My husband is not the father. I love the father of my child.

I cannot simply get a divorce. The man I love is wanted by the RIC.

If I'm not careful I will be shunned by the church and possibly everyone else.

If I change faith and become a Protestant, what will that mean? I imagine I will be shunned by the Church and again possibly everyone else.

I will talk to Eve again she thought. At least she can see the funny side of things.

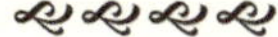

Kieran and Denny escorted Pat to Cobh.

Pat was informed that he was being given a second chance with his life and to remain in service with the Brotherhood.

There will be brothers on the ship and in America he was told. Mol wanted to avoid him blurting everything out to a RIC Constable. "Make him feel he is a valuable member," she said.

Pat was in steerage and was housed in large, shared dormitory-style space in the lower decks of the ship. His bunk bed was one arranged in a row, three tiers high, he had no personal space.

His privacy he felt was non-existent. He was disgusted that men, women, and children were sharing the same area. He found the ventilation was poor, leading him to suffer stuffy and uncomfortable conditions, particularly during rough seas. His food was basic, bread, soup, porridge, and potatoes. He had to sit in a large communal area.

Many people he encountered, were immigrants travelling in groups, and the shared hardships, he noticed, fostered camaraderie. He heard and saw that passengers held a mix of hope and fear, as most had left behind everything familiar and were embarking on a journey to start anew.

The length of the journey Pat discovered, was to take 7–10 days, and dependent on the weather and with the bloody war going on, there was a risk from U Boats, passengers were being informed.

He was greatly outsmarted he thought bitterly.

He needed to clear his head and start thinking logically.

Doing things hastily cost him, he thought.

Alice was the primary cause of all his trouble. He should have let Jimmy and her off to hell. Wouldn't he be better off now? Jimmy's sister Eve was a good-looking girl. She would have jumped at the chance to marry him.

He was sitting with a new acquaintance.

He asked his new friend if he could write a letter on his behalf. The gentleman was only too happy to have something to do.

He lifted his jar of ink, unscrewed the top and set it beside him. He took the pen from his bag and slid its nib onto it. He unrolled the sheet of paper, dipped the pen into the ink and started.

Mr Pat Flaherty

Husband.

25th day of November 1915

To the Most Reverend Father Michael Clarke.

Subject: Petition for Ecclesiastical Guidance on Marital Deception and Child Welfare.

My wife is Mrs Alice Flaherty & the child Master James Flaherty.

Your Excellency,

I write to you as a troubled man, seeking guidance and resolution for a matter that has deeply affected my conscience and my household. It is with a heavy heart that I must inform you of the circumstances under which my wife and I were joined in marriage, and of the subsequent challenges I have faced.

Before our marriage, I was unaware that my wife was already pregnant with a child conceived by another man. This grave deception was hidden from me until after our union was solemnised. I entered into the marriage in good faith, believing I was forming a proper and moral family under the laws of God and the Church.

Since the revelation of her deceit, my trust has been profoundly shaken. Compounding this distress is the manner in which the child, not my own, is being raised. I believe that my wife is failing in her duties as a mother. The child is neglected in both moral and material ways, and I fear for their spiritual and earthly welfare.

As a man, I have sought to uphold my vows, but this situation weighs heavily upon my soul. I appeal to the wisdom and authority of the Church to advise me on how to proceed in accordance with its teachings. If an annulment of this marriage is warranted under Canon Law due to the fraud and lack of proper consent, I humbly request your guidance in initiating the process. I deem my marriage to be null and void and am informing you that the sham marriage was never consummated. If you therefore decide to take action, your success will be greater if the marriage is voided.

Furthermore, I seek advice on how best to ensure the welfare of the child. While not my own, the child is innocent in this matter, and I feel a duty to ensure they are properly cared for, even as I questioned my ability to remain in the household. I couldn't remain after the deceit bestowed upon me. I am on my way to America as I write, to take a break and get my head clear.

I entrust this matter to your care and judgment and will abide by the Church's counsel. I thank you for your time and understanding and remain committed to acting in accordance with the teachings of Our Lord.

Yours respectfully in Christ,

Pat Flaherty.

The letter was folded and placed in an envelope.

The new Pat was going to be smart and make anyone that dared cross him pay dearly. Nobody saw Pat write the letter.

He chatted casually with the writer, congratulating him on his excellent way with words.

"Could you post that for me, please?" Pat asked. "I don't have any money."

"Of course, I will, my friend."

Pat wanted no one to see him with the letter for fear it would be confiscated.

❧ ❧ ❧ ❧

Pat's letter was opened by Father Michael one month later.

He called to see his bishop stating urgent concerns. He handed the letter to him.

"This woman's pregnancy is believed 'illegitimate'," he stated once he had finished reading.

"Her adopted family, I know, are upstanding people," the priest started. "They will most likely want to avoid any public shame and moral scandal. Pete and Kate Flaherty, Pat's parents will prioritise maintaining respectability and I believe will want Alice to be taken away to avoid gossip."

"Abstain from referring to her Christian name," the bishop said. "She has no Christian morals.

I will obtain a court order and have her removed to Bohermore."

෫෫෫෫

Alice and James were watching the stones being placed near where the mason was working on a gable wall.

A horse drawn carriage could be heard coming along the road and slowed at the Flaherty gateway.

The carriage was driven by a local hackney Pete Malone. Father Michael along with Constable Coleman Casey was seated on the back.

Jimmy slipped away and hid when he heard the carriage slowing.

Casey hopped off the carriage and approached Alice.

Father Michael stepped down, stood and stared at Alice.

Casey handed Alice the court order. "I'm summoning you to this court," he said pointing to the letter.

"You are an unmarried mother and morally delinquent and you are a burden on public resources. You will now be brought before the local magistrate supervised by Father Michael who has petitioned along with his bishop for your removal."

Alice along with James got into the carriage not knowing what was happening. Alice's immediate concern was that they were there for Jimmy. She agreed to go along with this charade to get them away from where Jimmy could get arrested.

Alice was ushered into the courtroom with James clinging on to her.

Father Michael rhymed off what she was being charged with.

Alice stood speechless. The old judge said, "You are found to be guilty of 'immorality', and an inability to provide for your child. What is your recommendation to the court Father?" the judge asked, looking at the priest.

"I have requested a place at Bohermore, your honour," he replied with a facetious bow.

Coleman led Alice and her son out to the awaiting carriage. Father Michael stayed behind to speak privately with the judge.

❧ ❧ ❧ ❧

Pete, Jimmy and Kate sat in the kitchen.

"How did that happen?" Jimmy asked.

Pete said he wasn't aware of anyone knowing the circumstances.

"What do you mean?" Kate interrupted.

"I haven't heard anyone gossiping, is what I mean," he replied.

Kate said some women at mass said they hadn't seen Pat in a while. "Asked in a gossipy way, if you know what I mean."

"Alice spoke to some priest," Jimmy said, "about….," (he didn't want to say the word divorce in front of Pete), "matters of marriage. I can't remember if it was that Father Michael though."

"When Alice gets home, we will know more," Pete said.

"Pete Flaherty, do you know nothing at all? Once the church gets their claws into you, they won't let go. We need to do better than wait, or we will be waiting forever," she said.

❧ ❧ ❧ ❧

Alice and James stood in the cold harsh entrance to the Bohermore home.

James was wary of the people dressed in the strange costumes.

"They are nuns," Alice tried to explain.

Father Michael walked in behind them and escorted them to the entrance desk

A nun with a severe face sat at the desk.

"Name?" she snapped. "Date of Birth?"

Alice gave her date of birth.

The nun looked at her.

"The child," she snapped again.

This was the first time that she had started to worry. Why was she asking for this?

Alice complied and tried to be as helpful as she could so that it might go in her favour.

Alice was handed a dark coloured dress and was taken to an adjoining room. James tried to go with her but was stopped by another nun. He started to cry and was immediately told to be quiet.

When Alice returned James was gone.

"Where is my son?" she cried.

"Take her away," the nun with the severe face ordered.

Alice was taken to a small room containing a small bed with a chamber pot underneath. She looked up quickly when she heard her door being locked.

Alice was frightened and wondered: What will they do to me here? How will they treat my baby? Will we be safe? What will become of me? What kind of life can James expect? Will I ever be able to leave this place? I feel so alone. No one in my family wanted me, and now I'm here with no one to turn to. I've brought disgrace upon my family. They'll never forgive me for this.

Have I sinned so badly that this is my punishment? Will God ever forgive me? The nuns are probably judging me, just like everyone else did back home. I'll do whatever it takes to keep my baby safe. James is all I have now. Maybe James will have a better life than I ever could give him. I hope he grows up happy and loved. I don't care what anyone says, James is perfect, and he is mine.

Will they treat me like a human being, or just another sinner they need to reform? Why should love and a mistake make me a pariah? I only wanted to be happy. Maybe this is where I'll find forgiveness, where I can start over. I'll endure whatever I have to for James's sake. We'll make it through this together. Maybe one day, my family will take me back, or someone will show us kindness.

Her door opened hours later, and Alice was escorted to a small chapel.

"You will kneel and reflect on your sins and responsibilities through prayer," she was ordered.

"Behave well and you may be permitted a small meal," she heard the nun utter.

The next day Alice was set at scrubbing floors with another woman. They were almost constantly watched by a nun. She said her name was Monica. "Don't upset them," Monica said. "No talking unless you are asked something."

Alice had so many questions she wanted to ask. "How long are you here?" she whispered.

"42 nights," she thought was her whispered reply.

❧ ❧ ❧ ❧

Pete spoke to Mol about what happened.

Mol was aware but had said nothing.

Mol said she would speak with Father Michael.

❧ ❧ ❧ ❧

Pat wasn't happy.

He was one of a gang of men doing hard digging work in poor weather conditions. He wasn't popular with the other men. He didn't care. He didn't want to be here, he knew, was the reason why. He would return home to Ireland as soon as he could get enough money saved. He would not be bullied again.

❧ ❧ ❧ ❧

Mol waited to speak to Father Michael after Sunday mass.

He had the air about him that he knew what she wanted.

Mol asked him why he had taken a perfectly happy girl and her child away. "You married them," she said.

"Her husband informed us that he is not the child's father," he said.

"Pat, her husband in America," Mol said.

"That he is," the priest said. "We had correspondence from him enlightening us of his wife's wrongdoings. We uphold the law and the good faith," he went on.

Mol was taken aback. She might have known there would be some backlash from him. After all, he tried to kill her, Joe and Jimmy. She would have to come up with a way of sorting this even though she had other things on her mind.

ھ ھ ھ ھ

Pete and Kate sat down on Mol's request to hear what she had to say.

"We must persuade the church to accept that we are Alice's family. Further to demonstrating this we have to show that we can care for her and James. We will have to express contrition and comply with moral expectations in line with traditions. We will have to pay any outstanding costs or penances. We also might have to negotiate their release by compensating the church. We will most likely have to present evidence of our ability to provide a stable and moral home environment."

"What does this mean?" Pete asked.

"It could be a letter from Father Michael or another respected community figure vouching for our family's character and intentions. We could use intermediaries, like our doctor, solicitor or trusted community figure, to negotiate on our behalf. We could pressure the institution through social or political connections if they held influence in the community."

This avenue, Mol stated, would be more likely in cases where the family had significant standing.

"What we will likely come up against is that Bohermore, where I have been informed Alice and James are, might resist release if they believed that Alice's penance is incomplete. If we lack funds, negotiating release will be more challenging. Or, we have to consider if Alice herself does not want to leave, or if the institution viewed her as morally unfit to return to us, this could complicate matters."

Mol let that sit with her parents.

"Oh, one last thing," she said. "Pat caused all this. He wrote a letter to Father Michael."

❧ ❧ ❧ ❧

Alice's day started at 6am. Prayer and reflection was the start of everyday. After this she was taken by a small thick set nun to the front porch with her mop and bucket. She went to an outside tank to get water. It had had a layer of ice on top. Alice tried to break it, but it was solid.

The nun was getting agitated watching Alice. "Fill the bucket, you stupid girl."

Alice got the mop and started using the handle to pound the ice.

The nun moved in close to Alice and caught her by her hair. She pulled back and Alice went tumbling to the floor over the mop bucket. "Stupid, stupid girl," the nun roared.

Alice got up off the floor and with one swift movement punched the nun in the face.

The nun fell down, and Alice stood over her.

"Lay a hand on me again and you will never get up," Alice said with her eyes on fire.

❧ ❧ ❧ ❧

Pat boarded the ship bound for Southampton.

He had money. He had been sharing rough digs with eight other Irishmen. Watching everyone's movements he had noticed where they hid their money. He feigned illness this morning, took their money and quickly went to the port.

Pat had found out that Sir Neville Francis Fitzgerald Chamberlain was his man.

Pat had been taken to see a snooker tournament and had listened to two men speak about the game.

"He brought it back from India," one of them had said.

"He is responsible for lots of things including being head of the RIC." This was the bit Pat took interest in.

He had thought about little else.

ஜ ஜ ஜ ஜ

As Christmas neared, Mol was in attendance at an important meeting. She liked the level of caution taken to ensure secrecy and safety.

In ascendancy was: Tom Clarke.

Tom was an influential elder statesman of the Brotherhood and a veteran of earlier revolutionary activity, he was central to revitalising the organisation. He was a leading planner of the upcoming Easter Rising and worked closely with the younger activists to mobilise efforts for the rebellion.

Seán Mac Darmada

Sean was the National Organiser. He was instrumental in expanding the network and influence across Ireland. He worked closely with Clarke to plan the Rising and was deeply committed to the cause.

Padraic Pearse

Padraic was recently brought into the fold due to his inspirational leadership and his role as cultural nationalist through his work with the Gaelic League and he was a headmaster of St. Enda's School. He was the public face of the rebellion.

Joseph Plunkett

Joseph had become deeply involved in the military strategy and planning. He was in ill health but was a key Brotherhood figure and contributed to organising the Irish Volunteers to act as the Rising's armed force.

Eamonn Ceannt

Eamonn was a member of the Supreme Council. He was also active in cultural nationalism and played a pivotal role in planning.

Thomas MacDonagh

Thomas was another prominent activist drawn into the Brotherhood through cultural and political work, he became part of the inner circle planning the upcoming Rising.

James Connolly

James was not a Brotherhood member initially, his Irish Citizen Army collaborated with the group before he joined the Brotherhood. Now he was integrated into the leadership of the uprising.

The Meeting

The group discussed the progress on the drive for recruiting members, particularly from the Irish Volunteers and the Gaelic League. An update was given on acquisition of weapons and training men for the eventual armed uprising.

Connolly briefly spoke about international support, particularly from Germany, to aid the cause including a planned arms shipment. The plan was outlined.

"We will seize key locations in Dublin. Our units will take over strategic sites in the city, including Dublin General Post Office (GPO), St. Stephen's Green, the Four Courts, and other prominent buildings. The GPO will serve as our headquarters for the rebellion.

"We intend to formally declare Ireland's independence through a Proclamation of the Republic, which will be read aloud and widely distributed. On the day our brothers will instigate uprisings in the pre-selected areas of our country to stretch British forces thin.

"We expect a shipment of arms from Germany. The German ship Aud will carry a surplus of arms for us. The Rising is planned for Easter Sunday, 23 April 1916, the element of surprise will be key to our success."

The meeting ended.

Sean Mac Darmada called to Mol as she left. "Your lad has left the States we believe. Nobody in their right mind would stay after what he done to his fellow workmen."

He filled Mol in with all he knew.

❧ ❧ ❧ ❧

Pat boarded a train in Southampton bound for Birmingham.

He had discovered that the man he was determined to speak to owned a metal works business there and it was involved in the war effort. Chamberlain lived in the city in a place called Highbury Hall. It was described to him as a large Victorian mansion. He was determined he would find it.

∾ ∾ ∾ ∾

Eve met Coleman at the agreed rendezvous.

When he asked her to walk out with him, she had refused initially because of him being in the RIC.

Now she had agreed, having spoken to Mol. They strolled along the beach and chatted easily.

"Can I tell you something in confidence?" she asked.

"Tell me anything," he replied.

She told him the whole story about Pat and Jimmy. About the cart loaded with straw and how Pat was behind it all.

Coleman stood astounded.

She said that Pat had been in America organising support over there and that he tried to blame everyone else for his actions.

"He even tried to implicate his own sister, Mol," she went on. "His father and mother have basically disowned him because of his carry on."

Coleman thought about the time they had him in the station and realised now that they gave him an easy ride. Then he recalled the straw and cart tracks. How stupid we were, he thought.

"I didn't think he had it in him," he eventually said.

"Jimmy wouldn't hurt a fly," Eve said.

"Where is Jimmy now?" Coleman asked.

Eve was nervous.

"You do believe me about him, don't you?" she asked him directly. "I would die if anything else happened to him."

"I believe you but I would need to hear it from him too."

"He is working on the new cottage at Pete Flaherty's place," she said tentatively.

"Now," she asked, "what is to become of poor Alice?"

Coleman recalled the visit and removal of Alice and her child. He felt bad now.

"One thing at a time," he said. "That's a lot to take in."

❧ ❧ ❧ ❧

Pat arrived at the big house called Highbury Hall. This was as grand a place as he had ever seen.

The door was opened by a maid. Pat asked to see the man of the house.

"Have you made an arrangement?" she asked.

"I'm here on urgent business," Pat stated.

Another servant appeared at the door and told Pat to be off with himself.

Pat stared at him and said loudly he was here on an urgent matter.

A voice called from within house. "Can a man not get peace?"

He walked towards the half open door.

"What do you want?" Chamberlain asked.

Pat told him he had travelled a long way to relay important information about the Brotherhood in Ireland. "I believe," Pat said, "you are the person I need to speak to."

"This better be good," Chamberlain said.

Pat was taken into a study where Chamberlain went around a huge desk and sat down.

"Get on with it," he said to Pat.

Pat told him that he was a lowly farmer lad and he had been forced to take the cart to the RIC station when the ambush had occurred. He felt very sorry for the men that lost their lives and would do whatever it took to make amends.

Chamberlain was not impressed.

Pat saw this and decided to play his ace card.

"They have been to Germany," he started. "They have won sympathy there and the Germans have said they will send a shipment of arms."

Now he had his attention. Chamberlain sat forward and poured two drinks from a large whiskey decanter.

"Go on, my boy," he said.

"The Brotherhood has men on board a ship named Aud and that is due to drop anchor off the south coast of Ireland to be met by small boats. This is scheduled to happen sometime in January next year."

Chamberlain looked at the man in front of him.

Why is he telling me this? Is it a trick of sorts? Is it a time-wasting tactic?

"Why are you telling me all this?" he asked Pat.

"I refused to be part of their fight," he said. "And because of that they told me to get out of Ireland. They took me to the boat for America and watched while I got on it."

"What do you want from all this?" Chamberlain asked.

"I believe I would be an asset to the RIC organisation," he said.

"I know how they think. I want to see them destroyed, every one of them. I want to live in RIC quarters for my own safety," he finished.

Chamberlain called his butler. "Get the carriage for this gentleman," he ordered. "Give him two pounds for his journey."

"Report to the Sergeant in Clifton and he will do the rest," Chamberlain said to Pat.

૎ ૎ ૎ ૎

Coleman called at the Flaherty home.

"I want to see Jimmy," he said whilst removing his cap.

Removing the cap was seen as a friendly gesture. Pete called Jimmy and said to Coleman to sit down.

"What business have you with him?" he asked Coleman.

Coleman said he would prefer to speak with him alone as there had been allegations made against him, and he needed to be certain that Jimmy was innocent before he could attempt to have his name cleared.

Pete attempted to speak, and Coleman raised his hand. "Pete, he said, you have someone here that is prepared to see reason. You know that is in short supply with the organisation I am with, and with some justification going by recent events."

Pete left the room as Jimmy entered.

Coleman asked Jimmy to explain what had happened to him in detail. He asked if he had any involvement with the attack on the RIC station.

Jimmy answered and left Coleman in no doubt that Pat had covered his own tracks and had thought nothing of sinking Jimmy.

Coleman told him to keep a low profile for the coming weeks to give him time to try and set the record straight.

❧ ❧ ❧ ❧

Mol addressed her unit. They were to set up an ambush to be carried out on the 23rd of April. That was to give plenty of time to find the best location, place equipment, arms and personnel there at the ready so that coming and going last minute wouldn't blow their cover.

❧ ❧ ❧ ❧

Coleman hadn't been able to speak to his Sergeant about the mistake they had made with Jimmy. Tension was still high since the ambush and showing any sign of favouritism towards the perceived enemy could prove problematic. He was mulling over in his mind how best to approach it when Pat entered the station.

"I'm here to speak with Sergeant Brown," Pat said in a confident tone.

Coleman got up and walked toward him. "Are you indeed?" Coleman asked him.

The Sergeant approached and appeared as if he was expecting him.

"Come this way, Mr Flaherty," the Sergeant said to Coleman's surprise.

"I have received communication from Chamberlain himself," Brown started while Coleman and Pat stood in his attendance.

"We have intercepted the Aud with arms and ammunition destined for our enemies," he said. "It's thanks to you for this. You are to be based here with quarters assigned to you. You will be inaugurated into the Royal Irish Constabulary with a rank of Deputy Sergeant Flaherty. We are grateful for your input and are delighted to have you with us."

✎ ✎ ✎ ✎

Coleman cycled to the secret rendezvous to meet Eve. He was in a weird mood and couldn't shake it off.

Eve was there when he arrived.

"What's wrong?" she asked.

"I don't know what has gotten in to me," he said. "You won't believe what happened earlier."

He told Eve the whole story. Eve was without words. "What!" she exclaimed. "What sort of devil is he? How did he come by such information in any case?"

"I have to answer to him now," Coleman said.

Eve was keen to get away.

"I can't stay," she said, "I'm needed at home to help my mother. We can meet again tomorrow," she said by way of an excuse to get away quickly.

She rushed to the Flaherty house. Mol was there with Pete.

"We have to talk and quickly," she said to them. "He's back and we are in trouble now. He informed the head of the RIC about an arms shipment from Germany, it was good information and now he has been made deputy Sergeant of the RIC in Clifton."

"Boys O!" Pete said scratching his head.

This could jeopardise everything Mol thought.

Eve said he had been given quarters in the station.

"I must go," Mol eventually said. "He has no gripe with either of you, Jimmy needs to find an isolated place to hold up in until all this blows over."

♋ ♋ ♋ ♋

Father Michael received a letter from America.

He had written to a bishop in Boston where his cousin had been given a position in his house.

He had informed him about the availability of a two-year old child. Usual terms, he had stated.

Now he had a reply.

The bishop had a number of couples keen on taking the child. A cheeky request followed asking could the child be brought to America where the child could be seen. A photograph would be less appealing he had written.

Father Michael thought about this. He was thrilled with the thought of travelling to America but not with a brat of a child. He would go, he decided.

Next day he made arrangements for his masses to be covered by his young curate and made his way to Bohermore. He was surprised to be told that Alice was being held in confinement due to her striking a nun that was supervising her.

"Hard labour will straighten her," Father Michael said. "You have to break them like a horse. Break their wild spirit. Punish those around her for any little indiscretion. They will turn against her. Then and only then will you see results."

"Thank you for your wisdom, Father," the sister said.

"I'm here for her child," he said. "Can you bring him to me?"

The sister was of the mind to ask for more detail but decided not to, in fear of his wrath.

James was brought to him, and they left in a hurry.

The sister opened the logbook and entered 'James Flaherty removed by Father Michael on this day'. No further details.

❦ ❦ ❦ ❦

Pat was delighted with himself. He was clever. He was a man in an authoritarian position now.

He must exercise his power and make everyone aware that there was a new executioner in town and as such everybody must be respectful or else…

❦ ❦ ❦ ❦

Mol called a meeting in a small cave along the seashore. She spoke quietly and with urgency.

"My brother Pat is back," she started.

After she had filled them in with all they needed to know she said, "We are all in grave danger.

He knows little about any of you. First names probably. Nothing else. He knows me, I will go into hiding but I have someone that can pass information along to us. He will be determined to get results.

Our plan goes ahead."

❦ ❦ ❦ ❦

Eve and Coleman walked along the beach.

Eve was concerned about them meeting at all. "It's dangerous," she told him. "The connection between you and me could cause you to get on the wrong side of him."

"Pat, you mean," he said.

"Of course. Who else? He will be dead against Jimmy. He is liable to say anything. Remember he tried to get Jimmy framed for what he done."

Coleman told her not to worry. He was hoping the Sergeant would see through him eventually. Eve didn't press him for information. She would have to get his absolute trust.

❧ ❧ ❧ ❧

Father Michael and James were aboard the ship sailing for New York.

Two ladies stopped to speak to them and said, "What a lovely little boy!" "He is my sister's child," he said when he looked up at them. "We are going on an exciting journey, aren't we James?" The child just stared at the ground. "He is a bit overwhelmed with it all," he continued. "God Bless ye ladies."

"Isn't that lovely?" one lady said as they walked on.

❧ ❧ ❧ ❧

Pete sat opposite Kate by the fire.

"He has come back, you know," Pete said.

"Yes. He will turf us out, you wait and see," Kate replied.

"I was too hard on the other boys and too soft with him."

Kate stopped him. "He is bad through and through. No two ways about it."

❧ ❧ ❧ ❧

Pat had every Constable at the station watching for any group activity.

"If there are gatherings of more than two, arrest them all. Haul them in," he ordered.

He felt unable to mention Mol's name. He hoped with the information he had given about the sort of locations used for secret meetings that Mol would be pulled in or shot if there was a gun fight. He would act innocent and claim he didn't know.

If on the other hand he thought, if he was to say what he knew, he most likely would lose respect from the men. However, up to now there wasn't a trace of the bitch. His father and mother must know.

He will visit them on official business he decided.

ç ç ç ç

Alice was crying. It felt like weeks.

She was given bread and water once a day. She was locked away since the incident with the nun.

She cried for her baby. Why was the world so cruel to her?

When she thought these thoughts, she cried self-pitying tears. She must try and think of what the end of all this was going to be. Surely to God, they cannot keep me locked up like this. When the Virgin Mary gave birth, she wasn't married, she argued with God as if he was in the room with her.

Why God is it always us women that get punished?

She got no answer, but the questioning seemed to give her strength.

Yes, she asked, with more aggression in her voice - Why, Why, Why? We are judged to be the weaker of the sexes, yet we suffer for man's sins.

Alice decided she would apologise to the nun. Say she was truly sorry for what she done. Then she would get their faith in her and she would demonstrate that she was reformed.

Then, she thought.

ç ç ç ç

Father Michael and James walked with the crowd disembarking in New York. He would go directly to the bishop's residence. He had decided not to bother visiting his relatives. They, he felt, half laughed at him in his cassock. He did consider becoming more like priests he had seen in Galway city, some of them wore trousers with a black shirt and white collar. But he felt more comfortable and traditional in his flowing cassock.

✣ ✣ ✣ ✣

Pat was at his desk.

He felt that he was being avoided. He had noticed that the other men washed their clothes and hung them out to dry. Pat thought they were sissies. He had listened to a group of them discuss their teeth. They had proceeded to crush eggshells, add baking soda and mixed it into a rough paste. They had toothbrushes. Pat hadn't seen this carry on before. The brushes had wooden handles with horse or hog hair, the paste they made up was used as a dip before scrubbing their teeth with the combination of the two.

Any wonder ye are being outsmarted by the Brotherhood, he thought.

Pat's clothes smelled bad; his breath was equally so. He noticed it himself. It's this bloody station. Everyone is squeaky clean. No cow shit, no manure, no healthy sweat, he would have to adapt he decided.

✣ ✣ ✣ ✣

Eve laughed until tears ran down her cheeks when Coleman told her that everyone was avoiding Pat.

"He is stinking," Coleman said innocently, and Eve laughed harder.

Coleman watched her face; she was beautiful in his eyes. She kept him at arm's length and that made her more attractive. He thought he would leave getting heavy with any talk of marriage until there was a clearer path for them. Jimmy was still in danger, and he hadn't been able to clear his name.

"I went to Bohermore," Eve said. "Can you believe that they wouldn't let me see Alice? She is in chapel reflecting, and she is not permitted visitors. I asked to see James her son and they refused that as-well. Poor Alice."

Coleman grew more attached to Eve the more he listened to her. She cared about everyone else, and he wished at that point she would care a bit for him too. I will have to earn it, he thought.

Eve said she wanted to tie wild horses to the bars on the windows at Bohermore and burst Alice out. Coleman loved this side of Eve. She had all these wild ideas.

He started thinking maybe this was the way to win her heart. Alice was dear to her, and she was hurting knowing that Alice was in a place she didn't want to be in. There were people doing far worse and not getting punished. However, breaking Eve out was not the answer.

❧ ❧ ❧ ❧

Father Michael and James arrived at the bishop's palace. What a statement this place made! Here was a man with power. The entrance itself was a masterpiece. Such elaborate grandeur. He stood back and admired it all. He had read books about the varying styles of buildings. Romanesque Revival architecture, popular for ecclesiastical buildings. He admired the pointed arches, steep gables, and intricate stone carvings dominating the façade.

This structure he imagined would have been built from locally sourced limestone and granite, that he surmised, gave it a sense of permanence and gravitas. The stonework included detailed tracery, sculptural embellishments, gargoyles and religious motifs.

He looked around and up at the large stained-glass windows depicting biblical scenes.

Next, he looked up at the steeply pitched roof, slate-tiled, with small spires and crosses, emphasising its ecclesiastical being. The grounds, he noticed, included manicured gardens, hedgerows, and a small chapel surrounded by wrought-iron fencing. This place exuded a sense of reverence, dignity, and authority.

He was taken into a waiting room. He was getting annoyed already. He hadn't travelled all this way to be shown into a waiting room like a common person.

The servant girl was pleasant. She chittered freely as if she hadn't a care in the world. He wouldn't permit that cheek.

She asked if they had travelled all the way from Ireland. He had no intention of answering her. "Leave us," he said, "we must pray."

He had expected the bishop to open the door to him.

He was livid after two hours passed. He had been offered tea but declined. His temper wouldn't permit. He heard a carriage pull up outside and at least two people approached the door. They were in the hallway outside the room when he heard the bishop's voice. He heard their voices trail away and again he was in silence.

After a few minutes the door opened and the servant girl informed Father Michael that he was to follow her. He was shown into a grand room.

The bishop was dressed in civilian clothing to his horror. Two other people were in the room.

They had eyes only for the child.

Father Michael was asked to be seated, and he again was offered tea. He wanted to scream. He felt like a delivery boy having delivered something and was waiting for a morsel of gratitude.

"Now," the bishop said, "this is the boy I told you about.

You will be asked to pay Father Michael's travel costs both ways from Ireland, costs for care to the home and a donation to our charitable organisation.

May I suggest 10 dollars for expenses and a donation of 50 dollars?"

Father Michael watched the couples' faces. They were clearly shocked with this sum of money.

"We believed we were helping this child," the lady said. "We didn't come here to buy the infant."

The man spoke now. "What is this?" he asked. "Should you not be compensating us for taking the little fellow?"

Father Michael wanted to say something but decided he would wait and see what transpired.

Within an instant the couple were ushered out the door.

The bishop never flinched.

"Father, how was the journey?" he asked.

An hour later a second couple were shown into the room. They were in their mid-forties, Father Michael estimated.

The lady focused on the child while the bishop and the gentleman made small talk.

Now the bishop started again.

"Let's cut to the chase. There are costs to date with travel and care expenses. A donation to our charitable foundation also. Have you considered this?" he asked looking at the man.

Father Michael was trying to work out what the man did for a living because he and the lady were exquisite in their attire.

"We are more than delighted to pay for any expense and of course a fine donation for your worthy organisation. The little chap will have a good home with us. Will two hundred dollars be acceptable?" he asked looking at the bishop.

The bishop reached for a decanter on his desk. He poured two large drinks for himself and the man.

Nothing for Father Michael or the lady.

James sat with his head down. He had adopted this pose ever since he was pulled away from his mammy.

The next day Father Michael was given his fare home and ten dollars to be donated to Bohermore.

"We are doing God's work," the bishop said to him as he closed the door out behind him.

James was taken by carriage with the couple.

؇ ؇ ؇ ؇

Joseph and his wife Liz had been unable to have children of their own and eventually decided to adopt a child. Liz, a devout woman, had confessed to her priest and he had told her he would make the necessary arrangements for them.

Now here they were, she thought. She would first and foremost get their doctor to call and check the child's health.

She made the call and waited. James wasn't friendly towards her, and she was unsure about what she should do.

The doctor arrived and after tea with Liz where they had discussed the adoption, he said, "Let's see the little fellow."

He undressed James and spoke kindly to him.

"This child is malnourished," he said with shock on his face. "He must have been in those soiled clothes for ever," he went on. He tried to turn him over, but James screamed. "Now, now," the doctor said, "I'm not going to hurt you."

The doctor could see the reason why the child was frightened but decided that it would be best not to say. He got Liz to put a blanket around the child and they went and sat down.

"You have a lot of hard work do here," he started. "This infant has not been given food or he has refused to eat anything he has been given. He has sores from being in soiled clothing for weeks it appears. What you must do now is, build his trust in you and your husband. He must see and hear kindness all the time to build that trust. Bathe with him. He likely has never seen a bath. Eat with him slowly. I will prepare a tonic for him and bring it back."

∾∾∾∾

The uprising was set to take place.

Mol and her unit were positioned in Lucan on the edge of Dublin.

Units were set up around the perimeter of Dublin to slow the British military's advance to the Four Courts where the main uprising was occurring.

Mol was keeping her unit buoyant after the news about Roger Casement being captured after landing in County Kerry. Today however

Mol related to her unit that approximately 1,200 Brotherhood personnel had just seized key locations in Dublin, including the General Post Office.

"Padraic Pearse has proclaimed the Irish Republic outside the GPO. We have caught the British off guard," she told the excited men.

Mol and her men fought to slow the inrush of British military forces to the city centre. The following day British reinforcements got through in large numbers and fighting intensified.

Good news was filtered back to Mol. "We are holding our positions across the city, including the Four Courts, St. Stephen's Green, and Boland's Mill."

The next message received was not so positive. "British forces have started using artillery to shell our positions and are causing significant damage to us."

The following few hours saw fighting spreading to other parts of Dublin, with civilians caught in the crossfire.

On Thursday 27th April, message received said, "Our position at the GPO was heavily shelled. Fires have broken out, forcing our men to evacuate."

Pearse and his men had relocated to Moore Street but were increasingly surrounded. On Saturday, Pearse was under such intense pressure that he ordered a surrender to prevent further civilian casualties.

Mol was downbeat with the message that the Uprising was over after six days of fighting.

$$\wr\wr\wr\wr$$

Three weeks later, Mol was informed that over 3,500 people had been arrested, and 90 brothers were sentenced to death.

Mol took letters from those to be executed. Pearse handed her a letter to be given to his mother.

Mo mháthair daor

Beidh an scéala cloiste agat cheana féin faoina bhfuil tarlaithe anseo. Táimid tar éis troid láidir a throid agus theip orainn. Tá áthas orm go bhfuil cónaí orm chun caibidil ghlórmhar amháin eile a fheiceáil curtha le stair na hÉireann. Beidh áthas oraibhse, freisin, as seo, agus beidh an bhrón a bhaineann le scaradh, cé go bhfuil sé searbh, ag smaoineamh go ndearna do chlann a ndualgas.

Tá litir ar leith scríofa agam chuig Willie, á fhios agam cé chomh dlúth agus atá sé aontaithe liom ó thaobh machnaimh agus meon. Faighimid bás go mairfeadh an náisiún. Déanfaidh ár gcuid fola an náisiún a athnuachan agus a athnuachan.

Níl aon eagla creidimh orm, agus níl aon droch-thoil agam ar aon fhear. Tá mé chun bás le breacadh an lae; Níl ach aon eagla amháin orm - nach fiú mé iad siúd atá imithe romham. Guigh ar mo shon, a mháthair ionúin, agus ná bíodh do smaointe ró-mhór ar an mbrón. Abair le Margaret agus Mary agus na buachaillí cuirim mo ghrá chucu. Inis Uncail chuimhnigh mé air; Feicfidh mé athair sula bhfaighidh mé bás.

Do Mhac

Pádraic

My dear mother

You will already have heard the news of what has happened here. We have fought a strong fight and failed. I am glad to have lived to see one more glorious chapter added to Irish history. You, too, will be glad of this, and the grief of parting, though bitter, will be tempered by the thought that your sons have done their duty.

I have written to Willie, knowing how closely he is united with me in thought and sentiment. We die knowing that our nation may live. Our blood will rebaptise and reinvigorate the nation.

I have no religious fear, nor have I any ill will towards any man. I am to die at dawn; I have only one fear, that I may not prove worthy of those that are gone before me. Pray for me, dear mother, and let your thoughts not dwell too much on the sorrow. Tell Margaret and Mary and the boys I send them my love. Tell Uncle I remembered him; I will see father before I die.

Your Son

Pádraic

Mol's eyes filled with tears as she read the letter.

Go raibh maith agat a chomrádaí as creideamh a thabhairt dom inár gcúis chóir

Oíche mhaith a chara

Thank you, my comrade, for giving me faith in our just cause.

Good night my friend.

ॐ ॐ ॐ ॐ

Father Michael went to Bohermore and handed over two pounds for the costs associated with the child. He didn't give the sister a chance to speak. He asked if Alice was changing her attitude.

"She is greatly improved," the sister informed him. "She is ready, we believe, to mix with the other mothers and contribute to meaningful work, thanks to your guidance, Father."

"Did she sign the papers?" he asked.

"No Father, she refused to do so."

"Keep her in confinement until she does so" he said sharply.

ॐ ॐ ॐ ॐ

There was great celebration at the station when news of the executions came through. Everyone was in a jolly mood except Pat. He had lost his usefulness he felt. The Brotherhood was defeated.

The Sergeant had told him to go to the barrel and clean up initially, then the next day in-front of others, he had said, "Jesus, man would you bloody wash yourself? You smell like a pigsty."

Pat was incredulous. The others watched his fall from grace. He needed to find a woman to clean his clothes and needed to adopt sissy habits if he was going to stay at the station. He went home.

"Mammy" he said as he entered the kitchen.

"Hello son" Kate replied with little surprise.

"How have you been?"

"Ah sure, you know yourself" was her reply.

Pete had seen him come along the road and followed him in. Pete didn't speak.

"Hello," Pat said in his direction.

"What do you want from us?" Pete asked.

"Nothing at all. Mammy might wash my uniform" he said half-heartedly.

"Might she indeed" Pete said.

"It's not much to ask."

"You will leave this house because your mother nor I want you here" Pete said. "You have chosen to bring evil to this house. We have not rested with all the pain and sorrow you set upon us. Now go."

Pat couldn't believe he had the nerve.

He didn't even congratulate him on his elevated position in the RIC.

"I have achieved more in my short years than you two have done in your entire lives" he blurted out.

"I am a Sergeant in the Royal Irish Constabulary, and you hadn't the wit to notice."

Pete looked at him for a moment.

"You know son, I have travelled very little. I have worked this bit of wet ground. I married your mother and never laid a hand on her. I provided while your mother reared the children. I can walk amongst my neighbours and receive a friendly greeting from each and every one of them."

"We might be seen as simple people, and maybe we are. But I will tell you, we are proud, we are fair, and we will leave this world and not leave an enemy behind us.

"One day son, you will come to see what I mean.

Now leave us."

Pat turned and left. He hadn't been ready for the lecture from his father. To hell with them, he muttered to himself.

He walked up the road to Eve's home. She was a plain girl from a cottage but his calling on her would make her and her family feel privileged. He straightened himself and knocked on the door.

Eve's father opened the door and had a look of shock on his face.

"Is Eve home?" Pat enquired.

"Yes sir, I will fetch her for you."

"That's more like it," Pat thought. Call me sir. That's how my father should have addressed me.

"Pat Flaherty," Eve said when she appeared.

"Eve, how are you?" Pat asked. "Care to walk so we can talk?"

"Certainly," she replied.

As they walked along the road, Eve wondered what on earth he wanted. She hadn't long to wait before she got her answer.

"I'm of a mind to take you as my wife," Pat opened up straight to the point.

Eve was flabbergasted.

"Are you now?" she said. "Sure, aren't you already married Pat?"

"Ahh don't worry about that bitch, she tricked me into that. I can get that scratched from the record tomorrow."

This statement got Eve thinking about something else, but she must quickly get back to what this smelly gombeen was asking.

"God Pat, you have taken me by surprise. Before I consider your words, I would need to be certain that I wasn't walking out with a man that was already married."

Pat turned around on the road and walked Eve back. "You leave that with me," he said as he left.

Eve went to see Jimmy first. "I have news of sorts for you," she said. "Pat Flaherty asked me to marry him."

"Jesus," Jimmy said. "Are you mad? Aren't you walking out with Coleman?"

"I am she said. But that's not the news I want to tell you. I asked innocently, 'aren't you already married?' His reply was that I wasn't to worry about that. He would get that marriage scratched from memory. They were his words."

Jimmy was at a loss. "Why? Is that something you feel I might like to hear?" he asked.

"Well, think about it. If the marriage is no longer and you can somehow get Alice to marry you, your and Alice's child will be legitimate. They will have no grounds to keep Alice in that place."

"Jesus," Jimmy said. "How can I get married with Alice in that bloody place?"

"Leave that to me," she said as she left.

Next Eve went to meet Coleman. Coleman was delighted she had instigated the meeting.

"Sit down," she said to him. "Pat Flaherty proposed to me this afternoon."

Coleman looked at her with anger in his eyes followed by remorse. Had he been too cautiously waiting for the right moment and missed his opportunity? He was speechless.

She went on. "I would never marry that pig of a man if he was the last man on earth. My heart is yours, Coleman. I just wanted to tell you that I didn't refuse him."

"What are you saying to me, Eve? You have me tied up in knots."

She explained how he had arrived at their home and asked her father if she was at home.

"We walked a short distance when he laid it on me. I was about to tell him what I thought until an idea formed in my mind." She told him what she wanted to do. Hopefully get Alice out of that place with her child.

Coleman looked at her. He tried to stop the tears, but they came anyway.

"You are the kindest person I have ever met. You put everyone before yourself and I love you for it," he said.

"You love me?" Eve said.

"Yes, I do."

"I love you too," Eve said with a beaming smile.

They walked along the beach holding hands and laughed.

"I hope I'm not the cause of a civil war within the RIC," she said, and they laughed more.

❧ ❧ ❧ ❧

Mol opened the kitchen door and walked in.

"Hello," she said to her father and mother.

"Oh. We haven't heard tell of you in ages" Kate said.

"How are you Mol?" her father asked her.

"I'm doing fine," she said.

"Pat hasn't long left," he told her.

He told her all about the unexpected and unwanted visit. "He left with his tail between his legs," he said with a small grin.

"He is too important to wash his own shirt," Mol said. "Did he ask about me?"

"Never mentioned you," Kate told her.

"Things will be quiet for a while after the executions in Dublin, I expect," Pete said to her.

"I don't know," Mol stated, "the public are not happy about what the British have done. Things could get bad."

❧ ❧ ❧ ❧

Father Michael was pleased with himself. He had a little nest egg after the transaction. He would build on that. There was more money to be made. He would send someone in his place next time.

He looked up at the sound of a knock on the door.

"Pat Flaherty, come in and sit down." Pat was still wearing his uniform and felt he was an imposing sight.

"I will get straight to the point," he said. "I got married to that woman but as I told you in the letter, I was tricked. I want that marriage scratched."

"Well now," Father Michael said. "That might cost a bit, but I will see that it's done Pat."

"Cost?" Pat said.

"Yes. Two pounds for all the administration."

Two pounds, Pat thought. That's a lot of money. Eve would certainly come with a bit of a dowry.

"That's ok," Pat said. "I will bring it along tomorrow. Can it be done as quickly as possible as I intend to remarry?"

"Yes," Father Michael assured him.

Pat got up and left.

Father Michael was grinning from ear to ear.

"Money," he said. "Just keep it coming." He thought, 'I will announce a special collection for myself at Sunday mass.' He was on a roll.

He fetched the books with the marriage entries.

He flipped open the pages until he found the names.

He wrote across the page,

MALADE MARRIAGE

Father Michael had read this term in a book by James Joyce called 'Dubliners'.

He left the book open so that he could show it to Pat when he presented with the money.

⍦ ⍦ ⍦ ⍦

Mol organised a meeting. She spoke to a packed room.

When questions were permitted, Denny, who was there with his younger brother spoke directly to Mol.

"There is a new political party called Sinn Feín. Would you consider running?" he asked looking around the room for some vocal support. The room burst into cheers and applause.

Mol was smiling.

She knew the party Sinn Feín was not directly involved in the rising, it had recently became associated with the independence movement.

Sinn Féin had branded itself as the political voice of Irish republicanism, advocating for an independent Irish Republic.

Mol was suddenly excited.

"Yes," she said to rapturous applause.

Beidh mé ag troid leis an peann seachas an claíomh ar son neamhspleáchas ár dtíre. Cabhróidh mé le fáil réidh leis an tír seo dár leatrom

I will fight with the pen rather than the sword for the independence of our land. I will assist in ridding this land of oppression.

෴ ෴ ෴ ෴

Pete, Kate, Mol and Jimmy were in the kitchen to listen to what Eve had to say.

She told of the encounter with Pat.

She said, "Rather than getting annoyed, this could be an opportunity."

They all listened intently.

"We have to get Jimmy and Alice married."

The buoyant mood became less so.

Kate spoke.

"How on earth can we expect that to happen?"

"Ok," Eve said.

"Once the marriage to Pat is nullified, we must get proof from Father Michael, I can get that. We have to get a willing priest to marry them in the Bohermore chapel. We must bring the families to try and overwhelm them."

"That's your plan?" Pete asked.

"Yes," Eve said.

"You know Eve, you are an angel."

"I can ask Coleman to come too," Eve said. "If he wears his uniform, it might add weight."

ઌ ઌ ઌ ઌ

Pat called to see Father Michael and handed over the two pounds. Father Michael reached for the book and showed him how he had annulled the wedding. "I need proof for my intended," Pat said. "Can she come in and see that?"

"Yes of course she can," Father Michael said.

Pat was delighted. Things were going his way, he thought.

Pat called with Eve and walked out along the road. "I have that done now," he said to her. "Call in to the parish church and see for yourself."

"I will," she said.

ઌ ઌ ઌ ઌ

Pete called to see Father Michael. "There is an upcoming wedding," Pete said. "I do believe there is, Mr Flaherty," Father Michael replied. "And congratulations."

"Yes," Pete said. "I want you to marry them."

"That won't be possible," was the reply.

Pete knew this was coming.

"We want the wedding to take place in Bohermore so that she will see it taking place," Pete continued.

"My curate will perform the ceremony," Father Michael said.

"Very good," Pete said. "We will of course be making a donation to your fine work. I have money set aside and can give it to your curate." "That won't be possible, a curate mustn't handle monies," he said quickly. "You come and see me personally is how that is done."

Pete stood up and shook his hand. "That's what I'd prefer," Pete said as he turned to leave.

The wedding was planned for the following Tuesday. Six days away.

The guests invited were:

Eve's parents

Her brother and two sisters

Coleman Casey

Pete and Kate

Mol

Jimmy and Joe

Connor Flaherty was home for a surprise visit from America. Mol and Connor left early for Galway.

They found a public house and went in.

There were several men already drinking stout.

Connor chatted easily to them.

Mol stayed out of sight as she would not be accepted in the public bar.

They left and watched for the guests to arrive.

Connor spotted Pat.

"Pat, my boy," Connor called out to him.

Pat looked surprised to see his brother.

"I couldn't miss your wedding. Come on and have a stout with me to celebrate."

The two men entered the public house.

Pat was greeted with great back slapping and shouts of 'the man himself'.

Pat was taken aback by how popular he was. This was his happy place. Bottles of stout were ordered and drunk. Connor ordered again.

Another man ordered and handed the drink to Pat. "Be-god-en I have to buy the great Pat Flaherty a drink. Sure, we heard mighty things about you." Pat was feeling that this is what he was missing.

&&&&

Mol, Pete and the young curate entered the Bohermore building.

The sister showed them into the small chapel. Alice was sitting in a pew with a nun alongside her.

Mol handed the curate her suggested order of service with a pound note inside. He looked at her for a moment before nodding approval.

The curate put on his vestments and prepared the altar.

The group entered the small chapel, all except Kate. She stayed at the reception area and waited until most of the nuns had filed in to enjoy the ceremony.

Kate had thought about her part carefully. Her own mother had tried to instil some wisdom when she was a girl growing up. She remembered being told to wear nice gloves to conceal your hands. Women especially were quick to notice if you were a working woman going simply by your hands. They would notice the roughness, your nails and general hardship just by looking at your hands. If you shake hands, offer the tip of your hand, keep the handshake gentle. A grab and shake would reveal the strength in your grip, again revealing that you were merely a working type.

Speak few words. Remember, empty vessels make most noise. Hold your head high and ask few questions.

Kate said to the only nun she could see, "We are very impressed with the work you do here.

My husband and I are considering a sizeable donation to aid your work. We are devoted people and as such are grateful for the service you are doing to our church."

The nun looked pleased. "We do our best."

"We rely on donations," she went on. "Sometimes however we don't get all that we should."

"Whatever do you mean?" Kate asked.

"Oh, I've said more than I should," she replied.

"What is your name?" Kate inquired. "In our correspondence we will mention your profession."

"Sister Tessa," she said.

"Would you be so kind as to give me a quick tour of the facilities, Tessa? I would be ever so grateful."

"Of course. Follow me."

The two ladies walked through the building where Tessa explained, "These are the mothers' dormitories. The washroom. The chapel is through there and the gardens, we grow all our own vegetables."

"And the children?" Kate said.

"Oh, they are down through here," and they walked. "You grow all your own vegetables, you say," Kate said, to deflect from the importance of seeing the children.

They arrived at a long window that divided the corridor and the room where the children were. They were being supervised by two nuns.

"Oh, this is good Kate," said while scanning the room for James. "And are there other children?"

The nun looked around the children, clearly counting them.

"18 there," she said, "that is all of them."

"Oh, replied Kate, I thought there would be more."

"The numbers go up and down," the nun said quietly. "Do you ever get attached to them Tessa," Kate asked her in her softest voice.

"I try not to," she said. "When they come, they clearly don't want to be here but when they are being taken they don't want to go."

"You have a lot of girls," Kate said.

"Oh yes, the boys are in more demand. We had a little fella go to America recently," she said quietly. "But I have said too much already. Please don't say I told you that."

Kate assured her by touching her arm gently. "America is a long way for a child. How did he get there?"

"I really cannot say. I would get in a lot of trouble."

"I'm only curious because if you were to go, I would want to make sure you travelled first class. I might even travel along so we could be company for each other. I have family in America you see."

"Oh no," Tessa said. "I wouldn't be allowed to go. Father Michael took him but mostly the adoptive parents come here and pick which one they want."

❧ ❧ ❧ ❧

Connor and Pat were laughing with the locals. They were drinking whiskey now.

Connor was telling him how clever he was to join the RIC. "I should have thought of that," Connor said "but then I don't have your cleverness."

Pat grew a foot taller every time he got a compliment. This really is a great day. "More whiskey," Connor ordered.

The curate said mass and then directed the wedding party to come forward.

At last, Pete thought.

"Do you Coleman Casey take Eve White to be your lawful wedded wife?"

"I do."

"And do you Eve White take Coleman Casey to be your lawful wedded husband?"

"I do."

"Do you Joseph Burke take Molly Flaherty to be your lawful wedded wife?"

"I do."

"Do you Molly Flaherty take Joseph Burke to be your wedded husband?"

"I do."

"And do you Jimmy White take Alice Duffy to be your lawful wedded wife?"

"I do."

"And do you Alice Duffy take Jimmy White to be your lawful wedded husband?"

"I do."

"I now pronounce you man and wife," he said three times looking at each couple as he did.

Kate was outside the chapel door as they came out. She watched the supervising nun move towards Alice and she quickly moved in and took her by the arm.

"Alice is a married woman now," Kate told her. "I am about to make a sizeable donation to your charitable work here. Don't spoil her day."

They spilled out onto the street quickly as planned.

It happened so quickly the nuns were left looking at each other.

Pat was very drunk. "I better go and get married now," he said to Connor, but Connor had left hours earlier when Pat had fallen asleep.

Pete and Kate's parlour was alive. The plan had worked so well. Pete singled out Eve and everyone agreed.

Kate was reluctant to mention James, but Alice did.

Alice hadn't stopped crying since she got home. She said she thought everyone had forgotten her.

"Are you sure he wasn't there?" she probed off Kate.

Kate went over again her conversation with the nun called Tessa.

Pete said, "Father Michael is bad news. Surely, he wouldn't have taken James to America."

Connor was a bit merry and was finding being in this group of people a bit tough, he needed to sleep off the alcohol.

His father was a new man. His mother was a lot smarter than he ever gave her credit for.

Eve White was a genius to organise the events today right down to the finest detail.

Mol spoke next.

She said, "I have a contact on the Cobh to New York ship. I can make enquiries because if Father Michael and James travelled that route they would have stood out."

Pete looked at his daughter and thought how on earth could she know such things.

෨ ෨ ෨ ෨

Pat staggered to the front door of the Bohermore building. He knocked and was greeted by the stern-faced sister. "Get away from here, you blaggard," she said to him.

"I'm getting married here," he stuttered.

"No more weddings today," she shouted and shut the door.

෨ ෨ ෨ ෨

Coleman went to work the following morning and announced his news as Eve advised.

"Make sure you tell them all that we have been courting for over two years. Because when he shows up, he will want blood."

Pat had gotten a carriage back to the station last night and his head was pounding this morning. He had fallen down several times and his clothes were in an awful mess.

Now he heard cheery sounds from within the station and he was reminded of the same sounds in the public house only yesterday. He was the top man then but wasn't feeling so today. He stumbled into the station from his living quarters and the place fell quiet.

"Hey up," he said. "What's the news?"

The Sergeant announced that Coleman here had gone and gotten himself married.

"Oh," said Pat. "And the lucky lady is....?"

"Eve White," Coleman said.

Pat's head did a somersault. "Eve married you? Impossible," Pat said.

"Sure, she was marrying me yesterday."

With that, the place erupted with laughter.

"You have a great sense of humour," Coleman said.

Pat started again, but the more he tried the more they laughed.

Everyone believed Pat had a sense of fun they had never seen before.

Then he lunged for Coleman. He caught him on the jaw and Coleman fell down. He stayed down while Pat was grabbed by two Constables. Pat roared down at Coleman that he was going to kill him. On hearing that the Sergeant indicated to have him put into a cell until he sorted this out.

১ ১ ১ ১

Mol was put forward to run in a by-election in Galway North in March 1917 and won the seat.

This followed the release of Irish republican prisoners in February 1917. Mol was aware that the party had restructured to represent a broader nationalist movement.

Eamon de Valera, was a survivor of the Easter Rising, and Mol was sure he would become leader of Sinn Féin at the October 1917 meeting.

Arthur Griffith had been the party leader following its founding in 1905.

She was pleased that the party formally abandoned Griffith's dual monarchy vision and adopted a platform advocating for the establishment of an Irish Republic.

Now the party began gaining ground in by-elections throughout 1917, capitalising on the decline of the Irish Parliamentary Party and the public's disillusionment with British rule.

Mol was now in the moving cogs of Sinn Féin which had become the umbrella organisation for various nationalist groups, including the Irish Republican Brotherhood and veterans of the Rising.

❧ ❧ ❧ ❧

Alice was angry. She had to find her son. Jimmy wasn't sure what he could do. "I will go to America and look for him," he told her. But she was inconsolable.

Eve called to see them. She saw that Alice was in a bad place.

"Ok," Eve said. "Let's talk this out. We have very little information at the moment. What we do know is that he is not in Bohermore. Father Michael took him away. The nun Tessa mentioned America."

Alice was starting to feel better. They all looked up to see Mol walk in. She sat down and took in what they were saying.

Then Mol said, "I have word from the ship. He travelled with a young boy and returned home only days later without him."

"Was the child James?" Alice asked.

"Most likely," Mol told her.

"The straightforward route is to ask him directly."

"He won't tell," Mol said.

"We could force him," Jimmy said.

Eve told them that James had to be taken there for a reason.

"My sister works in the school. She is friendly with the curate. He comes in to teach Catechism.

I could ask her to fish for information off him. We have to try and outsmart him."

❧ ❧ ❧ ❧

Sarah was Eve's sister and she was chatting to the curate Father Leo.

"Did you know Leo, that curate is Latin for care? And that you have the care of the parish?"

"Yes, Miss Sarah. I did know that."

"I'd love to travel," she said

"Where would you go?"

"America," she said. "Would you come and be my chaperone?" she teased.

"I might be going," he said.

"Stop! You!" she said in excitement.

"Yes. Father Michael told me that next time there was a trip there that I would most likely be the one to go."

"Oh, can I come too?"

"Now, now, it will be church business I will be going on."

"Church business, my eye," she scolded. "I never get to do anything exciting."

"Oh, come on Sarah. I am a curate. I cannot be seen with a pretty girl. What would people say?"

"We could say we are brother and sister," she said. "We would be apart when we get there if you have business to attend to."

"Stop it. You are assuming we are doing this, Sarah."

"But I like you. I look forward to your coming here every day."

"I am a curate, Sarah. Didn't you hear me?"

"Oh, ok," Sarah said and walked away from him.

ও ও ও ও

Pat was three days locked up now. He was like a caged lion. He gave that bastard Father Michael 2 whole pounds. Eve tricked him. All along she was going to wed that lad, Coleman. He felt like a nobody.

The Sergeant sent a telegram to Chamberlain asking for assistance with the problem.

He just received a curt reply stating that he was in a position of charge and to exercise his power to deal with minor issues such as this. He opened the cell door and told Pat to get out and not to come back.

ও ও ও ও

Eve took Sarah that evening to see Alice. Sarah told them of the conversation with Leo the curate.

Eve was impressed with her sister.

"I can get more information from him I believe. Me going to America was just aiming high," she said. "Mind you, I would go if I got the chance."

❧ ❧ ❧ ❧

Pat looked in the direction of Flynn's public house. He wanted to have a drink, but he remembered that they had refused to serve him a drink the last time.

He wanted to get his two pounds back from that bastard. He called to see Father Michael.

"Well, well, well, the newly married man," Father Michael said when he opened the door.

"What do you mean?" Pat asked.

"You got married, didn't you?

"You know bloody well I didn't."

Father Michael looked at him bemused. "Well, my curate preformed the ceremony."

Pat was suddenly embarrassed. The whole thing was a charade. Connor and the back slapping, all a bloody charade. I'm so bloody stupid. He turned and left without another word.

❧ ❧ ❧ ❧

Connor asked his father if he could talk to him.

"Of course," he said. "Let's walk, it's easier to talk that way."

Connor said, "I see a different man in you since I returned home. I only came back because I was so annoyed with Pat. Do you know what he has done?"

"I don't," Pete said, "and I'm probably better off not knowing". "Ok, well in that case, I won't say" Connor replied.

"If we could get along like this, I'd like to stay and work the farm if you would be agreeable."

"You know Connor, nothing would make me happier."

"We built Jimmy and Alice that little house and I think your mother and me could live in a small place like that so you could have the home house. If that would make you happy, son. I have something I want to give you for safe keeping. It was only when I thought I had lost it I realised that the man that gave it to me was a good kind man. I decided I had become hard and unlikeable. I don't want to be like that, son.

"Since then, I have found a new sense of worth. So please, son. Make your way here if you wish. We are family and we will look out for each other. I will sit down and write to the rest of them. I will apologise for being hard on them and tell them they are always welcome home here."

و و و و

Father Michael told the maid to fetch the curate.

"How did the ceremony go?" he asked when he entered.

"It was very exciting," the curate replied.

"There were three couples getting married."

Father Michael sat forward.

"Three?" he said.

"Yes. Let me think. Constable Coleman Casey married Eve White. Molly Flaherty married Joseph Burke and Jimmy White married Alice Duffy."

Father Michael swung a punch and hit Leo so hard he knocked him unconscious.

و و و و

Pete asked Kate to come to the parlour with him and Connor.

He told her about their conversation earlier and that he was going to write letters to the others to say they are welcome to come home whenever they wished.

Then he said he wanted to pass the gift he had been given on to his son.

Kate looked at Pete with tears in her eyes. This man has been absent for years but here he is now again. She got up and went to him. She kissed him on the cheek.

"I will fetch it."

Kate handed the box to Pete.

"We are giving you this," he started. "To look after and pass it on to your son."

He retold the story of its origin to Connor.

Connor bowed his head and said: "I'm glad I came home". "I'm glad I came home."

ع ع ع ع

Father Michael had to call to the doctor's home and ask him to come to the house as his curate had fallen and hurt himself. The doctor arrived soon after Father Michael had got back. His curate was not responding.

"He must have banged his head when he fell," the doctor was informed.

"This man needs to be taken to hospital immediately," the doctor said worryingly. "His skull appears to be fractured."

The local hackney was summoned. "He needs to be made comfortable, or he won't survive," the doctor insisted.

The doctor said he would go ahead to the hospital and make preparations for his arrival.

Leo was lifted onto the carriage by the driver and a helper. "God speed," Father Michael said to them as they left.

ع ع ع ع

Pat slept rough in a shed the past two nights. He was sore with the world. He wanted to kill somebody, something, anything. He wanted revenge against everyone. He decided to go back and see Father Michael.

He knocked at his door, and it was opened immediately.

"Come in Pat. Sit down. Have a drink." Two tumblers were taken from a press. Followed by a bottle of Powers' whiskey. Generous measures were poured into both tumblers.

Pat was more than surprised.

"You were right about the wedding," Father Michael said. "Only there wasn't one wedding but three.

Did you know about all three?"

"I have no idea what you mean," Pat said.

"Alice married Jimmy. Coleman married Eve and Joseph married Mol. You know all of them.

Were you not there with them?"

Pat told him he was tricked. His own brother had gotten him drunk, and he fell asleep.

Father Michael looked at him now.

There was another child to be delivered to America. He was going to send the curate this time, however that might not happen now.

❧ ❧ ❧ ❧

Kate waited outside Bohermore to catch sight of Tessa. Eventually she saw her.

"Ach hello, Tessa. How are you?" Kate said.

"Hello, Mrs Flaherty," she replied.

Tessa wasn't a bit awkward so there must have been no trouble.

"Would you care to walk a bit?" Kate asked.

"Of course. I'd love that," she said. "I like to walk in the evenings. What's on your mind?" Tessa asked.

"Alice says she didn't give permission for her child to be taken away from her."

She let that sit.

Tessa opened with, "It's not right what they are doing but we just follow orders you see."

"Do you have any idea where they took the child?"

"I don't. I will tell you if I find anything out that might help. I want to get away to America out of here. Too much sadness," Tessa said.

Word spread that the curate was in hospital and after school Sarah went to see him.

She wouldn't have recognised him, and she wanted to laugh at the sight of his head wrapped in bandages. Only his eyes were moving and then tears started coming out of them.

She took his hand and whispered, "What did you go and do to yourself?"

He squeezed her hand and drew a shape on her palm. She looked at him and wondered what it meant. She opened her satchel and removed a copy book and a pencil.

She laid it in front of him and put the pencil in his hand. "I WILL TAKE YOU TO AMERICA WITH ME," he scribbled.

Now it was Sarah's turn to have tears stream from her eyes.

ɷ ɷ ɷ ɷ

On Saturday morning Mol and Connor were drinking tea when Eve and Sarah called in.

Connor got up to stand, as a mark of respect. "Would you like some tea?" he asked.

"I'm Connor," he said to Sarah.

They took tea and Eve said, "We are slowly making progress."

Kate came in and sat with them.

"I saw Tessa last evening," she told them. "She said there is no record of James being taken away. She promised she will keep me informed if she gets any further information."

"He is planning to go back to America with another delivery," Sarah said.

"If Tessa keeps us updated one of us could follow them."

"I will do that," Alice said as she entered the room.

"I could go with you," Connor said.

Sarah looked at Connor. He is not as funny as Leo but he is a kind man she thought.

Sarah said how Leo had a cracked skull and could only move his eyes but had written that she could go with him if he was ordered to go next time.

"Is the curate's name Leo?" Connor asked.

"Yes," Sarah said.

❧ ❧ ❧ ❧

Connor took the gift from his parents out of its box. He opened the covers to reveal the insides.

He was fascinated with the movement. So intricate. He found himself enthralled with the movements of the workings within the watch. The movements that occurred and led to other mechanisms to turn and click. His brain was fascinated.

He thought about this. The rivers, wind, rain, gravity and petroleum, of course. He missed the noise of cars and trucks in America. There is none here at all, he mused.

He went to see Jimmy.

"Will you come to Cork with me?" Connor asked.

"I will when I get the jobs done," Jimmy replied.

"No. Not today," Connor said.

"Will you come to Cork?" Connor asked his father. "Jimmy and myself are going."

"Don't ask, just come," Connor repeated.

"I will so," answered Pete.

❧ ❧ ❧ ❧

Connor went to the Bank of Ireland and asked to speak to the manager. He had to wait but was eventually seen. Connor explained his plan and wanted a loan of £1000. The manager looked at him as if he was a madman

"What collateral do you have?" he asked.

"Nothing," Connor replied.

'No' was the answer.

Next he went to the Ulster Bank. He asked the same question with an outline of his plan.

"A thousand pounds, you say?"

'No' was the answer.

Next, he went to the Hibernian Bank. Again, Connor had to wait to be seen.

After he set out his plan he was asked about his background and marital status. He was asked if he had ever been in trouble.

"I will approve the loan," the manager said, "and what's more I would like to be your first customer."

Connor left with a spring in his step.

❧ ❧ ❧ ❧

Pete, Jimmy and Connor headed off to Cork.

The Ford factory was brand new. Pete stood marvelling at a Fordson tractor.

A gentleman approached them, and Connor asked to see the manager. When they were all sat in the office, Connor outlined his plan.

"Great, we'll we be happy to accommodate you, Mr Flaherty. There will be an opening of account for which you will need to deposit 75% of monies for stock and thereafter a top up when you order new stock. Do you have telephone?"

Pete and Jimmy were thinking that Connor must be joking around when he said what the order was to be.

3 motor cars and one Fordson tractor.

On the road home, further plans were made. The forge opposite Flynn's public house was vacant since old Bob died.

"If we can buy that, there is living quarters upstairs. We can then clean it out and get it all ready.

We will see about the telephone. We have the manuals here to learn about the workings."

Jimmy asked why he was brought along. Pete wanted to ask the same question.

"You will be the person that knows how to repair any breakdowns and they do break down.

Daddy, you must get the iron monger to make us a petrol tank."

❧ ❧ ❧ ❧

Jimmy studied the petrol 4-cylinder engine.

A handheld shaft was inserted here, he had his finger on the spot.

You swing it around and that causes the crankshaft to turn. Valves open here and gasoline is squirted into the chambers. A spark from this ignites the gasoline causing combustion.

"What's combustion, Alice?" he called out.

"I don't know," Alice replied.

The cooling system. Water cooled, using a manual crankshaft-driven fan.

Carburettor. To mix fuel and air for combustion.

Ignition.

Coil ignition systems.

Alice watched Jimmy trying to understand it all.

"Draw it out with a pencil," she said. "Remember what Connor was saying about something must be done in order for the other things to follow. When that is turned what happens?"

"Ok," Jimmy said. "Let me try that."

❧ ❧ ❧ ❧

Coleman and Eve were walking on the beach. Pat was kicked out of the job, he was telling her.

"No knowing what he will do now."

Eve told him about little James likely having been illegally adopted in America.

"What do you mean, illegally?" he asked.

Well Eve started. There was no permission given by Alice. She must sign away her rights to James, we are told. Can you investigate that?" she asked.

Coleman would do anything for Eve. "I certainly will," he said.

"The church believe they are a law onto themselves," he went on. "Father Michael is a crafty customer."

⁋⁋⁋⁋

Kate was 49 years old. She felt healthy and with her husband Pete's recent kindness they were getting along great. So much so Kate had a feeling she remembered having before. Surely this couldn't be happening.

She cycled to a village to see a renowned midwife named Laura. Women loved her especially because of her unusual name and it being Latin for victory.

Laura chatted to Kate and teased out what she needed to hear. She asked her for a urine sample.

The culmination of details along with the colour of her urine was enough.

"You are pregnant, Kate".

⁋⁋⁋⁋

Connor, Jimmy and Pete spent days preparing the area for the delivery of tractors.

The gasoline tank was being constructed, with an area inside the yard for assessment. A tap in the tank allowed for dispersal to a quart can prior to the motor car.

⁋⁋⁋⁋

Coleman spoke privately to his Sergeant. "I have a suspicion the local clergy are up to no good. They cannot simply remove children from their mothers without permission."

"Weren't you part of that charade with the Duffy girl?" the Sergeant said.

"I certainly was. But I was acting as an overseer of the law."

"That is not the issue I'm concerned about. Well, if we want to pursue this, it would need to be at local level."

"Why?" Coleman asked.

"Because if we try at a higher level, they will most certainly close ranks to protect the church.

They hide behind the church, all the churches, not just the one. People are very connected to their faith. Having huge numbers of people following the church is their ace card. People in huge numbers would come out and say things like the church did her a favour. She wasn't even married. She should thank the Lord someone else is taking care of her illegitimate child. That's what I mean, Coleman. So, if you want to, go at the people involved. They will likely get frightened, and you might get it stopped or put right."

Coleman was impressed with his wisdom.

෬ ෬ ෬ ෬

Pat watched from a distance his father, Connor and Jimmy.

He wondered what they were doing.

He wanted the watch. He had been thinking about how he was going to get himself back in the race. The watch was worth a small fortune. He would move to Dublin maybe. Buy a house and live it up.

His father was a new man. He envied Connor and Jimmy.

Now the three of them were laughing about something. Him probably.

The noise was heard from a distance. People stepped out of Flynn's and nearby buildings. Now there was a crowd of RIC men standing out.

Then they saw the motor cars followed by a loud tractor coming along the road.

Connor stood out on the roadway. Pat thought the fool was going to be run over. Then he saw him raise his arms as if to stop them.

The convoy slowed and turned into the yard. They turned around inside the yard and they lined up facing the road.

'Well, I never,' Pat said to himself. 'The bastard has my watch sold.'

There was great excitement. Pete didn't know how to stop himself smiling.

Jimmy was eager to see one actually working rather than his rough drawings.

෨ ෨ ෨ ෨

Coleman knocked on Father Michael's door.

"Come in," he heard.

Coleman entered and sat down without waiting to be asked.

"Father Michael," Coleman began, "I'm being told you took Alice Duffy's child away from her without her consent. I want you to show me the consent letter or return the child to its mother.

I will give you two weeks before I return."

Coleman stood up and walked out the door.

෨ ෨ ෨ ෨

Kate had been through all this before, but it was eighteen years ago.

Now she had to do it all again. She didn't really care what people would think, but she did at the same time.

'You know,' she told herself, 'it will be lovely to have a baby all over again.' She wouldn't tell Pete yet, she decided.

෨ ෨ ෨ ෨

Mol was put forward to run in the 1918 general election.

She felt she had found her joyful place. Women were not well represented, and she had to be on the ball to keep the male dominance as an advantage rather than it being an obstacle.

❧ ❧ ❧ ❧

Father Michael was at Bohermore. He demanded to know why Alice Flaherty had not signed the papers.

"Is her signature on any documents?" he asked perplexed.

"Yes. We should have," the sister said.

"Yes. Here, she signed the marriage registry."

"Give it to me," he said angrily. "Give me a consent form."

He took both the register and the consent form and left.

❧ ❧ ❧ ❧

There was great excitement at the yard. People came to see the motor cars and the beautiful tractor.

Pete forgot all about the everyday farm chores, he wanted to be here watching it all happen.

The sound of the car starting, the smell of the smoke from the exhaust, the horn and of course, the one fella that knew everything about motor cars.

❧ ❧ ❧ ❧

Sarah sat with Leo.

His bandages had been removed and scars to the back of his head were visible.

He was still in some pain he told her but not so bad.

"How did you fall?" she asked.

He told her what he remembered happened and then nothing.

Sarah looked at him with a solemn stare in her eyes. "He punched you. What for? You did nothing wrong. You were told to do the ceremony, and you did. There is something wrong there," she said.

"Did you know he took Alice's child away without her permission?"

"No, I didn't," he said.

"I'm not cut out for the church, I don't think anymore. I like being in your company too much."

"Oh, stop it," Sarah said. "Leave the church, your parents would disown you."

Not if I told them the things that go on here," he said.

❧ ❧ ❧ ❧

Pat had seen enough. He had to have used my watch to do all this.

He went home to confront his mother about the injustice. He found her in the kitchen.

"Hello Pat," she said when he walked in.

"Did Connor sell my watch to buy all that baloney?" he shouted.

"Sit down, Pat," she replied. "You know your father was given that watch as a gift when he was only a boy. He could have sold it many times over the years. There were times we had barely a scrap to eat.

But he didn't. That watch was much more than a gift. It gave your father a confidence that is hard to explain. He foraged his way through life knowing that someone had thought enough of him to give that gift. All the time he possessed it he felt he was only minding it. He held it dearly.

"When he thought it was lost, he felt lost. However, when I handed it back to him he changed. Getting it back made him look at what he had become, and he didn't like that. He looked around him and saw that he had pushed everyone away. I watched his face, holding the watch and I saw the boy that had been given that gift. 'Look after it,' he was told. It was like he was being told to look after life itself.

Whatever path you take, look after those around you. He looked after the gentleman that day in Dublin many years ago.

"He had driven Connor away. But Connor came back. Your father saw himself in Connor, a kind willing boy that had been given as a gift to all of us and he thought he had lost that. But he hadn't. It was where he had left it."

Pat wasn't interested in all this shit.

"The watch should have been given to me. I'm the one that stayed here. This house and the watch are mine."

Kate never moved.

"There is a path for you Pat, I'm sure of it, but for the life of me I cannot think what it is.

Why did you not stay a while in America?"

"I was pushed out. This is where I belong. This is what I choose."

"But Pat, there is nothing here for you now. What you did to Jimmy was wrong, you must see that.

You are going from one troublesome decision to another. What would you like to do with your life?

Moving away from here was meant as a kind thing for you. Most people find themselves when they leave. Have you thought about that?"

Pat felt the rage starting to boil within him, he was getting nowhere here. What was he to do?

Just then Alice walked in.

"Oh," Alice said. "Have you returned my son?"

"Don't speak to me, you filthy bitch," was all Pat could think to say.

"You sold my son, didn't you?"

Pat wasn't interested, bemused with what she was saying.

"What are you talking about?"

"You and the priest. How much did ye get for little James?" she said sarcastically.

"You are talking rubbish."

"Well, where is he?"

"You wrote to Father Michael, didn't you? He had me and James put into that place and now I'm here, but my child isn't. So, my guess is that you found a buyer for a child in America, you contacted Father Michael and he did the rest."

Pat pulled back a chair and sat down. He sat in silence, processing what Alice had just said.

"I admit I have been a pure cunt. I can but apologise," he said looking at Alice.

"I have done terrible things all out of jealousy and revenge. I haven't made a decision that has stood to me. Now I'm sitting in front of my mother and ex-wife and am utterly embarrassed.

I have to start now and try to make things right. I got a man to write that letter to Father Michael whilst travelling to America. That was wrong I see now. I really don't know if I cared about the consequences. What you have just said mother about the kindness shown to daddy makes me think that if I had been wise enough to show people kindness it could have made me feel better about myself.

But all I seem to carry inside me is bitterness. I cannot remember the last time, if ever, I said a kind word about anybody or anything."

Alice walked over to where he was sat and put her arms around him.

"Let's start today," she said. "What you just said Pat took a lot of courage. Would you believe me if I told you that it made me feel good?"

"I need to see Jimmy. Will he kill me?"

"No," Alice said.

"I need to make things right with Mol. I need to see Coleman. And I need to speak to my father."

❧ ❧ ❧ ❧

Leo wrote a letter to his bishop outlining that he wanted to resign his position because of loss of faith.

He decided against going into any more detail.

He had gone to his parents and explained what had happened. They argued that Father Michael was only one man, and he should consider asking for a transfer elsewhere.

His mother thought there was an additional reason for him wanting to leave.

"It's your decision at the end of the day. We will support you as best we can."

A week later he received a response from his bishop.

"I have received your letter and am deeply saddened to learn of your intention to resign from your sacred office as a priest of the Church.

"The priesthood is not merely a role but a divine calling, a commitment made not only to the Church but to God Himself. I urge you to reconsider this decision in light of the eternal consequences and the spiritual needs of your flock.

"If you are struggling with doubts, temptations, or difficulties, I encourage you to meet with me personally. Together, we can seek the grace of God to strengthen you in your ministry.

"You must understand that such a decision would have profound implications for your life, both in this world and in the next. Consider carefully the responsibility you have undertaken and the scandal that may arise from such an action.

"Should you persist in this course of action, I must inform you that I will need to refer this matter to the Holy See. Until then, I urge you to suspend this decision and continue in prayer and reflection."

❧ ❧ ❧ ❧

Father Michael looked at his handiwork. He couldn't see any difference between the two signatures.

The door knocked and he said, "Come in." He was surprised to see his curate walk in.

Leo waited to see what he would say.

"You have recovered from your fall."

"I have," Leo said. "I have written to my bishop," he started. "I have asked to resign."

"And your reasons?" Father Michael asked.

"It's not for me," he replied. "It's not who I am."

He had thought about saying he wanted more from life but that could be an indication that he had seen something or someone that he wanted. He let what he had said sit.

"Well now," Father Michael said. "This is unusual to say the least. Go and get everything ready for the rosary tonight," he ordered.

Father Michael took down a thick book and opened the index page.

He scrolled down until he came to:

Role of the Holy See.

He became agitated when he saw the word investigation.

He read:

Any resignation from the priesthood or request for laicization needs approval from the Holy See.

A bishop can handle minor disciplinary matters, but significant decisions, especially involving the dispensation from vows, require Vatican involvement.

The Holy See will aim to maintain the integrity and authority of the priesthood. It will undertake detailed investigations and justifications before accepting resignations or granting dispensations."

Holy God, he thought.

❧ ❧ ❧ ❧

Eve saw the lady cycling by the house and thought she looked familiar. She jumped on her own bicycle and followed her down the road. Sure enough, she wheeled into Flaherty's house.

Kate opened the door to Tessa. She told Tessa it was a wonderful surprise to see her. Eve opened the door and walked in.

"I'll make the tea," Eve said.

Kate would have liked to have chatted to Tessa on her own, however she liked Eve a lot and was eternally grateful for all she had done for Alice.

Eve told Tessa she was a great woman to cycle all the way here.

"Sure, I'm delighted to get out. I must confess I had to tell a little fib as to where I was going. My mother wasn't very well, I had lied."

"I'm sure you will be forgiven," Kate said smiling.

Then she told them about the visit from Father Michael.

"He is up to no good, I think. He was mighty cross with the sister that works in administration.

He took the marriage registry book and the certificate that Alice signed with him."

Eve walked across the way and called Alice.

"Come quickly," she said.

Alice listened to what Tessa said. "The bastard," she blurted out, "sorry, sister,

I didn't mean it."

"It's ok," Tessa said. "Please call me Tessa."

Mol came out of an adjoining room with a bundle of papers in her arms. She had heard the exchange.

"Will more than one of the sisters in Bohermore say that Alice never gave signed or verbal consent for her son to be given up?" she asked, looking at Tessa.

"Oh, I don't know," was her response.

"Why more than one?" Alice asked. Eve answered that it would be his word against one sister, and he would get his way. That's why.

"Exactly," Mol reiterated.

"Do the other sisters ever speak about Father Michael?" Kate enquired from Tessa in a gentle tone.

"Yes. None of us really like him because he is very condescending towards us. We make funny faces behind his back," she went on. "But we are all afraid of him really."

"We could write to the bishop who is his superior I suppose," Eve said.

They all looked at Kate for wisdom.

She said, "They will stick together there is no doubt about that. Have any other children been removed?"

"No," Tessa said. "Not since little James."

"We have a very difficult situation here.

If he produces a consent paper with Alice's signature, then we could be beaten."

Pat knocked on the half open door and said, "Excuse me I just need to speak with my sister."

Kate said, "This is my son Pat and this is Tessa from the home in Bohermore."

"Pleasure to meet you," Pat said.

Kate wanted to make Pat feel involved in family matters so decided to tell him why Tessa was here and the concern they all had.

"If I might speak," he said. "Certainly," Alice said.

I went to see Father Michael a while back after the weddings in Bohermore.

"He said, 'Have you been to America?' I said yes. He said I might have you go again but cut off before saying anything else.

"I had reason to go back and see him again a short time after that. He was a different person that time," Pat went on. "He was on edge about something. If it is agreeable to everyone I could go and see him again and see if could I find out more."

❧ ❧ ❧ ❧

Mol said, "I will walk out with you now," to Pat. "What's got into you?"

"I want to make things up with you and everyone else," he started. "I have been an awful person and if given the chance I will try to become a better brother to you."

"Pat, you are impossible to read."

"I was in a very crazy frame of mind. I drove everyone away with my jealousy and spiteful thoughts.

When I heard you address the meeting, I should have been proud but instead I resented you.

When I saw Connor setting up his enterprise, I should have been there to help but instead I wanted to destroy it. When Jimmy told me he was going to go away with Alice I should have slapped him on his back, instead I tried to kill him. Even if it's not here Mol, I'm going to try my best to make up for my behaviour."

Mol kissed him on the cheek and said, "Well-done Pat. That took courage."

⚜⚜⚜⚜

Pete was pleased that Pat had seen the error of his ways and asked Connor if there was work here, he could be given.

"No," was Connor's answer. "Reputation is very important, Daddy. If we take Pat in now our reputation could take a bashing. We must grow our name in the business first."

Pete was annoyed but only briefly. "You are right, of course, son," he said.

⚜⚜⚜⚜

Alice loved the smell of oil off Jimmy when he came in from his work. She told him all about the day when Tessa had called.

"Will we ever see our son again?" he said.

"We will," Alice said. "If it's the last thing we do."

⚜⚜⚜⚜

After reading the response from the bishop, Leo decided to speak to Father Michael.

"I have requested leave to resign," he said to Father Michael when he was admitted into his room.

"I don't foresee any resistance from you, Father."

"Do you think you can bully me?" Father Michael responded sharply.

"It's up to you."

"If you want there to be an investigation well then, block my request." With that Leo turned and left the room.

༄ ༄ ༄ ༄

On December 14, 1918 Mol was running as a Sinn Feín candidate in the first general election held after The Great War and the Representation of the People Act 1918. This act Mol was thrilled with because it significantly expanded the electorate. In Ireland, now, women who met property qualifications could vote for the first time.

Mol wasn't happy with all of the restrictions against women, but it was a move in the right direction at least.

Women had to be 30 years or older to vote whereas men could vote from age 21.

Women had to meet one of the following criteria:

Be a property owner (owning property of a yearly value of at least £5), or

Be a tenant (occupying land or premises with a yearly value of at least £5).

Be the wife of a man who qualified under these property conditions (even if she did not directly meet the property requirement herself).

Mol was elected and had the breakdown in her hand.

Party Seats Won

Sinn Féin - 73

Unionists - 26

Irish Parliamentary Party - 6

Mol won the seat with a significant majority, securing 7,835 votes against her opponent from the Irish Parliamentary Party, who received 3,509 votes.

Mol kept with the party line that despite being elected, she joined Sinn Féin's policy of abstaining from Westminster and instead pulled ahead to participate in the First Dáil Éireann, to be convened in January 1919.

જ્જ જ્જ જ્જ જ્જ

Connor just sold the second motor car for two hundred and fifty pounds. The last of the three that had been delivered was reserved by the manager that gave him the finance.

Now he wanted to order another batch.

The telephone was a contraption that took getting used to. Pete was totally bemused by it and many from the small place had come to see it.

The tractor had been a hit with lookers but no buyer. Sure, the horse can do as much, they said.

Connor would go back to Cork.

He had seen Sarah in the village a few times and thought he would ask her to walk out with him. He thought she might refuse him because she hadn't shown any signs of liking him. He would ask anyway he decided.

He walked to the school gate and waited there. When the hustle and bustle of the rushing children had passed him, she appeared.

"Oh, hello," she said.

"I was hoping you might let me walk you home," he said. "I could carry those," nodding towards her books.

"Well now," she said with a cheeky smile. "It took you long enough to ask."

They chatted about the children, the weather, the election and then he said, "I have to go on a trip." He watched for a reaction but got none.

"It's only down to Cork," he said. "I was wondering if maybe you would care to come."

"Oh now. Well, isn't that an invitation?" she said.

"All above board, of course," she said looking at him.

"Oh, of course. Can you get a day or two off?"

"Your timing is good," she said. "Did you not see the excitement of the children? That is them on holidays now. So yes, I will go with you."

☙ ☙ ☙ ☙

Pat called to see Father Michael.

"Good to see you, Pat," he was greeted. "You are looking well. What have you been up to? I haven't seen you at mass."

"I'm not much good at the auld masses, Father, to be honest with you. I'm trying to get myself sorted out. I'm looking for work and hope to start looking a bit beyond here. A bigger town maybe. There is not much around here. I might even go back to America."

"Have you any dealings with your family?"

"Ahh, not at all. Sure, they had their fill of my bad behaviour and now I just leave them be."

"I will organise a bit of work for you. It will mean delivering a child to an address in New York. Is that something you would consider? Your fare there and back will be paid and a tidy sum aside."

"Ok," Pat said. "Just let me know when you want me to go."

Pat was bursting to give them all the news of what just happened with Father Michael.

When he got to the house Kate, Pete and Mol were eating their dinner.

"Sit down, son," Kate said, "I will get you something to eat."

"I'm ok Mammy," he said. "I have news."

"Does this involve young James?" Mol asked.

"Yes, it does."

"Ok, let me give Jimmy and Alice a shout."

He related the conversation with Father Michael. There was silence until eventually Mol spoke,

"Before you do anything be aware that since the war the American government temporarily requires all immigrants to carry a passport due to security concerns. This is part of the Passport Act of 1918.

"Prior to now as you would probably know, immigrants could enter without passports, but now, wartime restrictions have had them tighten border controls.

"You must get an Inspection Card. As you will be departing from Europe you will receive an inspection card from the ship's medical officer or port officials. This card will include your basic personal details and will confirm that you have passed a preliminary health inspection before boarding.

"Manifest Record: Ships are now required to maintain passenger manifests, which lists details about each traveller, including,

Name, age, sex, marital status

Occupation and literacy status

Last residence and intended destination in America

Names and addresses of relatives or friends in America

"All of this information will be reviewed at American immigration stations, Pat.

You and the child will need Health Clearance.

"Now you must undergo medical examinations at the ports of departure and arrival, Ellis Island. Anyone with a contagious disease (like tuberculosis or trachoma) will be denied entry.

"A 'clean bill of health' or verification of vaccination could be required," Mol told him.

"They will ask you for Proof of Financial Support. You will need to demonstrate you will not become a public charge. You will have to show evidence of financial means, a job waiting for you or family support in America."

"That a lot to take in," he said.

"I will help you get your paperwork in order," she told him.

"Jimmy said Alice will travel with you but separately if you get me."

"If we are seen together…"

"Absolutely," Mol interjected.

"We must have your documents ready too. I also believe we should have a set of documents for little James. That is hoping of course he can be found."

"You are brilliant. You think of everything. I wish I had a bit of your brain Mol," Pat said.

ھ ھ ھ ھ

Connor and Sarah cycled to the train station.

She was asking him all about motor cars. "Why don't you have one?" she teased him.

"I couldn't afford to have a motor car. Simple as that. Someday I will though."

Sitting beside her on the train was much nicer. She chatted easily but he felt he needed to relax and enjoy the moment. He asked her about herself and the things she liked to do.

Then he asked about Leo. "You and Leo get along great," he said.

She turned towards him and said, "Are you a bit jealous?"

"Hmm. Yes. A bit," he said.

She reached up and pinched his cheek. "Don't be," she said. "He is a bloody priest. We just laugh. Or I just laugh at his awkwardness. You see I think he doesn't know how to be around girls. He gets embarrassed and I find that funny."

"But does he?"

"What do you mean?" she asked.

"Does Leo find it funny when you laugh at his awkwardness?"

"No, he just laughs," she said in a quieter voice.

The train pulled into Kent station in Cork.

Connor told Sarah that the name Kent came from Thomas Kent, an Irish nationalist executed in 1916.

She laughed at this and said, "You should be teaching, not me."

Now he laughed. He stepped off the train and turned to offer her his hand as she stepped down.

He had been thinking about this opportunity and because she accepted it, he was now going to try and hold onto it. He needn't have worried. She linked into his arm. He was walking on air.

They walked to the Ford factory, and he delighted in showing her everything. He went to the Fordson area of the factory. He saw all the different implements that attached to the back end. He took a note of each one and then entered the office area. She was clearly impressed when a man approached and called out with an outstretched hand, "Mr Flaherty, welcome back."

The business was completed as quickly as Connor could, so that they could be alone again.

Later that day he took her to a boarding house he had arranged by telephone.

Sarah seemed pleased that he had been gentlemanly enough to have booked her, her own room.

☙ ☙ ☙ ☙

Father Michael arrived at his bishop's residence having been summoned. He was asked to wait which he recalled being annoyed about previously. Now he was happy to wait as he didn't know what was going to happen next.

"His Grace will see you now," he was told.

He entered to a reasonably pleasant greeting.

"Father Michael. Take a seat," the bishop said.

"Your Grace," Father Michael said taking a small bow and reaching to kiss the ring on the outstretched hand.

"Now. We have some unsavoury business to discuss," the bishop started. "Your curate. What sort of an idiot is that fellow?"

"I don't think he is cut out for it," Father Michael said. "His head is always somewhere else."

"Can't you discipline him? Get him to toe the line. Isn't that your strong point Father Michael?"

"Yes, Your Grace. Of course, I agree. But I have tried all kinds of things to get him to get his head right.

If I may, I would say we would be well rid of him."

"This is very unusual indeed. Did you and he not get along?"

"Well yes to a point. He seems to have made his decision."

"I'm going to send him to Lough Derg for a period of six months. I have made the necessary arrangements. He leaves in 5 days' time. He will continue with services until then. Now I have adoptive parents for three children. You will take them, of course. You leave tonight. So, go on your way now."

When he left, he felt he had come out of that really well. But leaving tonight. He has a nerve. No consideration.

And he thought it all out. 'I couldn't even say there was nobody to cover the services.'

He got to Bohermore as quickly as he could. He told the sister at the reception that he was taking 3 boys whose mothers had signed consent forms waiving their rights to their children.

Tessa couldn't watch the little boys be taken out so she got her coat and hopped on her bicycle. She called to the only sister she met. "I have to run for a quick message to my mother. She's not feeling well," and she was gone.

Two and a half hours later Tessa flew in the Flaherty door.

Out of breath and sweat dripping off her, she hoarsely spoke, "Three boys on their way to America."

Then she sat down. Pat handed her a glass of water. "Get Jimmy and Alice quick," she said to no one in particular. Pat spun around on the floor and was gone.

When he returned Kate said, "Get out of here."

"What!" Pat said exasperated.

"You cannot be here," she said. "Quick. Go and walk where he will be able to find you. Bring your documents with you."

"Ahh. Now I get you. Jesus, if only I had a brain."

෬ ෬ ෬ ෬

Mol was in Dublin. Sinn Féin had achieved a ground-breaking victory in the December general election, winning 73 of the 105 Irish seats in the British Parliament. However, instead of taking their seats in Westminster, Sinn Féin established their own government in Ireland, marking a crucial step in the struggle for Irish independence.

On January 21, 1919, Mol and her fellow Sinn Féin MPs convened in Dublin and declared that they were the legitimate government of Ireland.

Mol was in chambers for the first meeting of the Dáil Éireann.

This is a great day, Mol thought because at this inaugural session, they just issued the Declaration of Independence, reaffirming Ireland's sovereignty and repudiating British rule.

They agreed on a plan.

Sinn Féin were to begin establishing an alternative government to challenge British authority:

They encouraged local councils to align with the Dáil rather than British institutions.

They will set up courts to handle disputes, bypassing British judicial systems.

They agreed that these steps were part of building a functioning independent state.

The Dáil was to seek international recognition for Irish independence.

Éamon de Valera was to go immediately to the United States to garner support and funds.

❧ ❧ ❧ ❧

Connor and Sarah walked arm in arm along the banks of the river Lee.

"I've never had a girlfriend before now," he told her. "Oh, I'm your girlfriend. Am I indeed?" she said laughing.

"Well, I would very much like you to be," he said.

"I am happy to be your girl," she said smiling. She turned into him, and they shared their first kiss.

❧ ❧ ❧ ❧

Pat walked towards the chapel when he heard the motor car coming.

The car slowed down and eventually stopped. "Pat," Father Michael said, "I on my way to the train station, hop in."

Pat sat in and saw three children sitting on the back seat. "Isn't this lovely?" Father Michael said.

"It's a great invention to be sure," Pat said back. "You're off to America then?"

"I am."

"Have you all your paperwork?"

"What?" Father Michael said angrily.

"You know. The passport stuff. When I was there, they said the rules are all changing now for going to America."

Father Michael was relieved. He thought that must have heard about Alice's mess.

"I will sort all that out," he told Pat. "Will you bring my motor car back for me? I don't want to leave it at the station."

"I will," said Pat.

Pat waited at the station until he heard and then saw Jimmy and Alice coming, running. Imagine this is all my fault, he thought. And they forgave me without more than a second thought being given.

"Hold up," he said with outstretched arms. "He is going himself. I was talking to him. He didn't ask me to go. You cannot let him see either of you or he might get suspicious." Jesus, he thought, am I after saying something clever.

"You are right," Jimmy said.

"Put your scarf on, Alice."

"We will stay well away from him."

"Thanks Pat," Jimmy said as they left.

❧ ❧ ❧ ❧

Kate felt a cramp and she grabbed onto the end of the table. She felt movement most days now but today was different.

She got her coat and walked over to Alice, then she remembered they were gone. As she turned, she heard a motor car back at the house. She walked back to see Pat getting out of the car.

"Pat," she said, "could you give me a lift to my lady friend's house, I need to see her."

"Hop in," he said, "this is Father Michael's car. He asked me to leave it at the parochial house, but I decided that I might not get the chance to drive about very much. Tell me where she lives, your lady."

"Up this way," Kate directed.

Laura was about to get on her bicycle when they pulled up. "Thanks Pat," she said and nodded for him to go on his way.

Laura sensed that Kate was in need of her, so she set her bicycle against the wall.

"Come with me now," she said putting an arm around her. "Are you full term?"

"I believe so Miss Laura."

"Ok, let me lie you down in here and I can have a look. Ok, everything looks fine. I am just going to get a few things ready."

Laura delivered the baby 20 minutes later.

"You have a beautiful baby girl," Laura said.

"You are the kindest person," Kate said. "Thank you. Can I call her after you, please?"

Laura smiled and said, "That would be lovely."

৵ ৵ ৵ ৵

Pat was loving driving the priest's motor car.

He was in a good mood, but he didn't have a job and that meant he had no money. Yet here he was, driving around like a wealthy businessman.

He decided he would leave the motor car at the priest's house and think about getting work.

He drove the motor car in the back of the house where Father Michael had instructed. As he was getting out, he saw two large keys.

He took them in his hand and started thinking.

He was about to walk out of the back yard when he saw people arriving to the chapel for mass.

He went back to a concealed area behind the parochial house.

He has money, I know he has, Pat thought. It's like I am being told, here is your chance.

He started to weigh up the whole situation. Do I or don't I? Would anyone care?

The bell sounded.

Another sign he thought.

He inserted the key and turned it. Clunk. The heavy lock opened. He had an hour to find Father Michael's ill-gotten gains. He searched drawers, bookcases, boxes and coat pockets. He sat at his desk. His heart was pounding. Take a few deep breaths he said to himself. He pushed the chair back and looked beneath the desk, another drawer, this one locked. He went to the door he entered from and withdrew the key and returned to the desk. Click, it opened. He slipped the drawer all the way out and placed it on the desk.

Marriage registry, he saw on top.

He removed that and saw papers beneath. There was Alice's name.

He lifted those out and there was a neat cigar box. It was heavy. He lifted it and set it on the desk.

He opened it to reveal at least twenty pounds. He replaced the cover and set it back in the drawer. He took the marriage registry book and placed the sheets of paper inside it. He replaced the drawer, locked it and lifted the book to take with him.

He locked the door and put the keys back in the car. He started to walk home.

❦ ❦ ❦ ❦

Connor and Sarah were at the station when they spotted Jimmy and Alice on the opposite platform.

"Jim," Connor shouted across.

Jimmy looked over and saw them. He didn't speak back but pointed ahead at something.

"They must want to meet us at the entrance," Sarah suggested.

The walked out to meet them.

Jimmy relayed the plan and said they couldn't delay because they wanted to keep Father Michael within sight.

Connor said he didn't think it was a good plan, but he was not going to try and deter them.

Jimmy and Alice walked briskly along in the direction Father Michael and the children were taking.

Connor and Sarah got onto the train heading to the West.

❦ ❦ ❦ ❦

Pat arrived home and entered the kitchen. His father and Mol were sitting, drinking tea.

Pete was still a bit uneasy around Pat.

"Pat," Pete said. "There's tea in the pot. Any word of your mother?"

"I left her off at a lady's house this morning."

Mol looked at him. "What lady?"

"The midwife woman."

Pat then set the book down on the table between them.

"I had the priest's motor car and was leaving it back to his house when I saw the house keys," he told them. "I decided to go into the house and get a look around."

Now they both looked at him.

"Jesus, Pat. Did you steal anything from him?"

"Just borrowed what is there between ye," he said. "I could have and I did consider it. There was a load of money in the same place as that," pointing to the book.

They both kept looking at him.

Then Mol opened the book. The sheets of paper had a bold heading:

Consent Form

By signing this document, you are formally relinquishing your parental rights, allowing your child to be adopted by another family.

At the bottom it had Alice's name and signature.

Mol opened the register book and saw Alice's signature. It was a reasonable match. She put the two signatures together and asked both of them to look.

Before they could answer Mol said, "We need Coleman Casey here."

Pat said he would fetch him, only he wouldn't go near the station. He hadn't been there since the day they put him out of it.

"I will go," Pete offered.

While he was away Mol said to Pat that he had done a good thing. "Not touching his money was also a good thing. We have to stay on the right side of the law at all costs," she said.

Pete returned with Coleman.

"Well, Pat and Mol," he said.

"Sit here, Coleman," Mol said to him.

They went over the goings on, and Coleman looked at Pat.

Then he said, "Put everything back exactly as it was."

He let that sit with them.

He took the consent page in his hand and said, "Except this one. We need to let Father Michael believe that he has the signed consent form."

"What about making a mess of Alice's signature?" Pat suggested.

"No," Coleman said, "distorting the signature would still leave him with a signature of sorts.

If I go to him, which I am due to do, I will be asking for the signed proof. He will present what he believes to be in possession of, but it won't be there."

"What will happen then?" Mol asked.

"You don't have the consent you need for the adoption to be legal, I will inform him and because of that I must insist that the child is returned to its mother."

Mol said, "I don't believe it's enough. There is a sister from the Bohermore home willing to say that Alice never signed her consent."

"If we had that kind of proof on their official document. Say headed paper, with a note stating that Alice Flaherty refused to sign a consent form it would certainly add weight. Put it back where you got it with the register book."

Pat loved this. He was in the company of great brains. Pete just listened.

Pat said, "I will go to Bohermore and speak with that sister Tessa." They looked at him thinking if there was any reason why he shouldn't be the one to go.

"Wait for her away from the place," Mol said. "She goes for a walk every evening."

"What's that?" Pete said.

He heard a noise outside. Kate walked into the kitchen and handed the baby to Pete.

"Her name is Laura," she said.

Pete looked at his wife and then down at the baby.

Mol stood up and put her arms around her mother.

"I thought there was something amiss with you lately but my goodness. It's amazing. Sit down and I will get you some tea."

❧ ❧ ❧ ❧

Pat waited for a long time but eventually Tessa came. When she got near, he called her. She recognised him but was a bit uneasy.

"I want to ask you for a note simply stating that Alice didn't or refused to sign a consent form, if you please."

She was very confused now.

Pat decided to tell her the whole story.

Tessa seemed relieved that a member of the constabulary was involved.

"Ok," she said, "I will get it ready, when do you need it for?"

"He said he would come back the next day at the same time and the same place, if that suited."

❧ ❧ ❧ ❧

Jimmy and Alice had a small bunk on the ship. They decided she would stay in the bunk to avoid Father Michael getting a glimpse of her. Jimmy, he wouldn't really know they thought. He had been keeping a watch for any sign of him and reporting back to Alice.

The ship was docking now, and they were anxious.

They didn't really have a plan. Connor had been right. They stayed back as people started to disembark via the gangplank. They inched forward and watched him in his billowing cassock go down the gangplank. Alice was broken hearted for the children. She watched them cling to each other's hands. Finally, they disembarked themselves and walked through the crowded streets.

ᴥ ᴥ ᴥ ᴥ

Connor was waiting on the delivery from Ford. He had got the surprise of his life when he saw he had a new baby sister. The house was full of joy. The little bundle was passed to eager arms and rocked from side to side.

Now he heard the noise of the engines coming. A truck carrying the tractor implements was first, followed by three Model T motor cars. He smiled as he recalled Sarah sitting in a new car and pretending she was driving.

Connor directed the lorry to a pulley wheel he had fixed in place for lifting heavy equipment.

Jimmy would be missed. One of the cars he had sold was back with a broken wheel following its being driven into a deep rut on a road.

A short letter awaited Connor when he had returned. "I would like you to acquire for me an Austin 20."

It was written on clergy paper, and the address was the bishop's residence.

That car is not available in Ireland he was sure but he thought immediately about another trip away with Sarah.

ᴥ ᴥ ᴥ ᴥ

Pat waited again for Tessa to appear.

He was deep in thought. He enjoyed having a thing to do. It was purposeful. He thought he was using all this as an excuse not to go and find a job of some sort. Tessa walked towards him with a letter in her hand. "There you are. Now go and get it into place. I will be in trouble but, I don't care."

"I know all about being in trouble," he said to her. "But you are doing a good thing."

He left and headed to the parochial house.

❧ ❧ ❧ ❧

Jimmy and Alice had followed Father Michael and the children for what seemed a long way.

"The poor little mites can barely keep up with that brute," Alice said.

They were in an affluent area now. They were both in awe of the size of the houses. When they had been in the port area it had been huge sheds, then small houses huddled together with children everywhere, now there were big houses and not a child to be seen.

They watched him turn into a grand house.

Now, what were they going to do?

❧ ❧ ❧ ❧

Father Michael knocked on the door of the bishop's palace.

The maid girl opened the door and let them in.

They were shown into the same room again. The maid offered tea, but he declined. "I will get the little ones something nice," she said.

"They are perfectly fine," he snapped.

"Oh, come on now," she persisted. "They will be much happier it they have a little something." He couldn't be bothered arguing with her.

❧ ❧ ❧ ❧

Jimmy and Alice were tired and hungry. "We didn't think this through at all. What are going to do now? If he took James here, how are we going to know."

They felt deflated. They continued to watch the door.

"I will go and find us something to eat," Jimmy said.

"I will stay here and see if anything happens."

Jimmy stood up and stretched. The door of the house opened, and a girl appeared, pulling on a coat as she left.

"You stay Jimmy," Alice said as she walked away, not giving him a chance to object.

Alice followed the girl to a shop a few hundred yards down the road and around a corner.

She watched the girl buy sweets. Alice bought a loaf of bread and called to her. "Hello, hi," the girl replied. "I'm Ali…" she nearly said her name. That could be a mistake.

"I'm so sorry," Alice said.

"I don't know what to say. My baby was taken from me and brought here to that house I believe. The one you came from just now."

The girl looked a bit stunned at first.

"Kathleen is my name. I am a maid in the house. I just cook and clean. Who are you?" she asked Alice. "I am Alice. I came from Ireland to see where that priest took my child."

"Look here now," Kathleen said. "I live about two miles away from here." She told Alice where the house was. "Go there. My mam will let you in. I will talk better with you when I get home from work. I must get back now."

≈ ≈ ≈ ≈

Pat waited for the bell to sound. He watched as people approached from all directions, on bicycles and on foot. He retrieved the keys and entered the house again. There was a letter on the desk placed where Father Michael would see it that wasn't there when he was here last.

He opened the drawer, removed it and placed it on the desk. Careful to try and remember where it had been, he set the book inside and returned the drawer to its position.

He locked the door on his way out, put the keys back in the car and left.

"Phew," he let out when he got clear of the house.

∞∞∞∞

Connor telephoned the Austin company in Birmingham. "I'm enquiring about an Austin 20," he said. He was asked to wait. A gentleman then spoke. "The 20 is not available just yet," he informed Connor.

"May I travel across to see one please?" Connor asked. "Yes, of course. Come whenever suits you."

∞∞∞∞

Jimmy and Alice found Kathleen's home. They knocked on the door and were greeted by a small set woman.

"Hello," she said.

Alice started to tell her about meeting her daughter and as soon as that was said the woman opened the door wide and told them to come in.

Alice was wary of people especially since her experience at Bohermore.

The woman said, "My name is Cecelia, but everyone calls me Cis. I came over here from Ballindine in county Mayo. Kathleen is my only child; she is a kind girl but she is a bit flippant."

Jimmy looked for any signs that there was a husband. There were no boots, pipe, tobacco, shirts. What else would only a man have about the place? He tried to think. Hmmm, no holy pictures or statues either. No hat or cap. Alice spoke and that brought Jimmy out of his trance.

"My baby was taken from me," she started saying.

Cis listened to the woeful tale.

Then she said, "I would likely have been in a similar place had I not asked my brother that was immigrating to let me come with him."

Alice admired her bravery and told her so.

"It wasn't easy," she said "but my brother was kind and that got me by."

"Kathleen tells me everything," she went on. "When she comes home you can ask her anything and she will tell you."

❧ ❧ ❧ ❧

Kathleen gave the children the sweets she had bought. Father Michael was annoyed with her for doing so.

"His Grace is ready to see you now. Shall I keep the children here?" she suggested.

"No," he snapped at her.

"Your Grace," Father Michael said when he entered.

The bishop ignored him as he was busy organising something on his desk.

"Yes," he eventually said. "Father Michael, how was your trip?"

"Very good," he replied.

The bishop hit a brass desk bell in his left and Kathleen appeared.

"Have they arrived yet?" he asked.

"Yes, Your Grace," she said.

"Well send them in."

A middle-aged couple were shown in to the room.

"Ahh, Mr and Mrs Bailey," the bishop greeted them.

"Take a seat."

One of the children Father Michael noticed was licking his fingers. That bloody servant girl giving them sweets, he thought annoyingly. He slapped the child's hand away from his mouth.

The man leapt up and said, "Don't be such a brute. A defenceless child. You should get on your knees and beg for forgiveness."

The man ushered the three children away from him.

"If Your Grace is agreeable my wife and I will adopt all three. We had intended to adopt one but honestly, I wouldn't want to leave any of these poor children in this man's company for another minute."

The bishop said that there were other couples desperate to adopt and that wouldn't be fair on them.

"Well," the man said. "In that case we will leave the three here with you and let the others not be disappointed."

"No need for that," the bishop said.

That was not the time to play hard ball he thought. He had to back track now.

"It would be nice to keep the three together. We can find suitable children for the other couples."

"Very well," the man said. "You will be expecting a donation of some kind."

"We hope to receive donations, yes."

The lady stood up and took out an envelope from her bag.

She handed it to the bishop and said, "I think you will find everything in order."

"Thank you," the bishop said.

"I will need you to come back for some formalities once I have them ready. Maybe in a fortnight."

The couple left the room with the three children.

The bishop looked at Father Michael.

"A timely slap indeed," he said. "Good work. Saves me having to go through the process with the others," he said grinning.

He hit the bell again.

"Tell the others I have been called out on urgent business and they will be contacted when they are to come back," he told Kathleen. "Very well, Your Grace," she replied.

He put the envelope into a drawer and took ten dollars from his purse. He handed it to Father Michael. "Now go and continue God's good work," he said.

Kathleen was standing at the front door waiting to open it and let him out. She knew the bishop wouldn't entertain him for long.

❧ ❧ ❧ ❧

Connor waited for Sarah to finish her day. He smiled broadly when she appeared. He loved the easy way she had. She handed him her books and linked his arm.

"Well, Mr Flaherty. How are you today?" Sarah cheered.

"I'm wonderful" Connor replied, " I am going to England and was wondering if you would like to come with me."

"Well, aren't I the lucky girl? When are we going?" she asked nudging him in his ribs.

"When you are not teaching?" he said. "At the weekend maybe."

"Ok," she said.

❧ ❧ ❧ ❧

Kathleen arrived home and met Jimmy and Alice. She told them about what she done for the bishop and what went on every day. Alice asked her if she had seen their son James.

"The last time that priest came that was here today, he had a little boy," she told them.

When she described him Alice burst out crying. "That was him definitely," she said. "Do you know where he was taken?"

"I don't," she said, "but there will be a record. He keeps records of donations received and the names of the people who made the donations. Sometimes there is large amounts of money involved. What do you intend to do if you find out where they have your son?" she enquired.

Jimmy answered, "We don't know."

"You are probably thinking of grabbing him and running," Kathleen said with concern on her face.

"The people that are adopting children have money," she told them. "And money gives them leverage.

"With the utmost respect for you, you don't appear to have their kind of money. You would need a carefully thought-out plan. The ships from here to Europe leave weekly and sometimes less frequently.

Your timing would need to be accurate. I would suggest you would need to be on the ship halfway across the sea before they would know the child was missing. Laws are strict here, if you were caught you could be put in jail for a long time.

"You are maybe thinking of talking to the couple. You could be lucky, but I doubt it. You are a mother; you have a mother's instincts. She will likely not. To them, you will be seen as vagrants looking to take their child.

"Another option would be to approach the bishop and explain that you never gave consent. Believe me, he would dismiss you with a wave of his jewellery laden hand. He would have ready answers. You changed your mind. You weren't fit then and are not fit now.

"Finally, you could go to the police force here. They would honestly look at you as if you had two heads. They are probably the busiest police force in the world. They simply wouldn't give you any time."

Jimmy and Alice were astounded with this young girl's wisdom.

"Stay here with us for a few days and then decide. I will get you the details you need in the meantime if I can. Sometimes he locks the door of his private quarters."

≈ ≈ ≈ ≈

Kate was listening to Connor about his trip to England. He was excited she could see and as soon as he mentioned that Sarah was going too she knew where the excitement was stemming from.

"I don't want to put a damper on you trip," she said, "but, would you take Pat along too?"

"Why on earth?" Connor asked.

"Because I want him away from here when that Father Michael returns. If any enquiries are made people will know he was off in England."

"This is to do with the switched papers?"

"Yes. He can do his own thing. It might be good for him. Please," she asked.

"Very well," he told her.

❧ ❧ ❧ ❧

Pete was showing a farm manager from the Big House the implements that connected to the back of the Fordson tractor.

The two-furrow plough. He was explaining how the socks were replaceable if it hit a rock and got damaged.

"That way you could adjust the depth you wanted to plough. Deep for spuds," he explained. "Less so for corn."

Pete was a mine of information about the different implements.

"This is a harrow and is attached in this way. This is a driller which can open and close drills.

And this box here attaches to the back, and you can carry all your tools around the farm."

A price was negotiated, and Pete and the farm manager parted ways to speak to their respective employers to see if agreement could be reached.

❧ ❧ ❧ ❧

Mol was in Dublin for party talks. Britain was attempting to introduce military conscription in Ireland, provoking widespread opposition. Mol and her party were playing a central role in mobilising resistance through the Anti-Conscription Campaign, earning broad popular support and aligning themselves with the aspirations of the Irish public.

❧ ❧ ❧ ❧

Connor, Sarah and Pat boarded the train for Dublin.

Sarah didn't seem to be bothered that Pat was travelling with them. "What do you like to do?" she asked Pat, an innocent question she often asked the children in school. She got a range of answers from the children.

A farmer like my daddy.

A priest like my uncle.

A schoolteacher like you, miss.

A train driver.

They were the usual answers she recalled.

Pat said he didn't know. But he had really enjoyed having driven the priest's car.

"I felt alive," he said. "It's simple really. I am no good at working out complex things like Connor and Mol can."

They got off in Kingsbridge Station and took a tram to O'Connell Street. Connor took them into Lyons's Tea Room for afternoon tea.

Sarah looked at home and Pat joined Connor in teasing her about how at home she seemed.

The boat across to Liverpool was heaving with people. They joined in with a group of lads playing cards and everyone shuffled up to let them sit down.

Sarah asked each one where they were going and what for. "Work," they all replied. "There's good money to be made." Their brothers or cousins were already there.

Sarah thought when she looked at these young men that most of her class would probably go the same route and what they learn in school will carry them along in life.

They got the train from Liverpool to Birmingham and walked to the Austin works factory. Connor was amazed with size of it in comparison to the Ford factory in Cork.

Sarah suggested that the two boys carry on and she would look around the town.

"It's a city," Connor teased. "One of the biggest in England, don't get lost now."

"There will be more of a chance of ye two bucks getting lost," she said as she walked away.

Connor and Pat were taken through the production line by a representative called Rob, to the finished motor car. "This is it," Rob said.

He mentioned the sale price starting at £450 going up to £800. "This is a different field entirely."

This car had a powerful engine and had luxury features beyond a man's dreams.

"Can you deliver it to me in the West of Ireland?" Connor asked.

"No. Dublin would be as far as we would go. We are setting up a depot there right now. Would that do?"

They discussed parts and the additional aspects that increased the price. He would need this detail for the inquiring client.

They left and went to meet Sarah.

❧ ❧ ❧ ❧

Father Michael returned and grumped as he walked from the train station. He wasn't getting the status from his bishops that he deserved. They expected him to do all the hard work. He had tried to speak to both bishops about having an intermediary person do the leg work but was instantly dismissed.

"This is important church work," he had been told. "We need to keep the circle tight."

None of this made him feel better.

He entered the yard now and retrieved his keys from the motor car. He was getting becoming impressed that Pat had left his motor car where he had instructed.

He entered his room and saw the letter. He sat down and opened it.

Dear Father Michael,

It is with a heavy heart and a weary pen that I write these words to you. These past months have brought me to a precipice of doubt, not in God, whose grace I still hold as my guiding light, but in the Church and, more specifically, in those entrusted with shepherding His flock.

My work here has become a trial, not because of the people, who remain steadfast in their faith despite hardship, but because of the attitude of our own leadership. Father Michael, you speak often of service, yet I find your actions fall far short of the ideals you profess. There is a coldness, a disconnection between your words and deeds, that grates upon my spirit.

The Irish people are suffering greatly, under war, conscription threats, and the grinding poverty that has long plagued this land. And yet, where is the Church in their hour of need? I had hoped to see compassion, to witness a living example of Christ's love. Instead, I have seen more concern for parish coffers than for the widows and children who lack bread.

Father Michael, you speak from the pulpit with a certainty I cannot match, condemning those who question authority or who seek a new course for this troubled nation. I have heard you belittle the aspirations of those who long for an Ireland free of foreign rule, calling them 'rebels' and 'agitators'. Is it not the duty of the Church to stand with the oppressed? Did not our Lord Himself say, "Blessed are those who hunger and thirst for righteousness"?

I feel trapped, torn between my vows and my conscience. I entered this life believing I could serve God and His people, but now I wonder if I am merely serving an institution grown too distant from the Gospel it claims to uphold.

Pray for me, Father Michael that I may find the courage to discern my path forward. I do not wish to abandon my faith, but I cannot continue as a silent witness to this hypocrisy.

Yours in Christ,

Your Curate, Father Leo.

❧ ❧ ❧ ❧

When Sarah arrived home, she had a letter. She sat down and opened it.

My dearest Sarah,

As I put pen to paper this evening, my heart is heavy with both dread and longing. I write to you not merely as a curate of the Church, but as a man, a man who finds himself utterly captivated by you, your gentle wit, your steadfast kindness, and the light in your eyes that seems to pierce through all the gloom of these troubled times.

I must confess a truth that has lain heavy on my heart for some time now. My vows, which once seemed so clear and sacred, now feel as though they bind me from the very life I am meant to live. My calling, I realise now, was not to solitude but to love, love of you, which has grown silently yet fiercely within me.

You may think me a fool or a coward for considering this path, but I would willingly leave behind the vestments and the altar if it meant I could walk beside you. The recent trouble with Father Michael has taught us both, I am sure, how fleeting and fragile life can be. How can I stand idly by, clinging to a life that no longer feels true, when the chance to share something so real and beautiful with you lies within reach?

I know the cost of what I am proposing, not only to myself but to you. This will not be an easy road. Society's judgment may be harsh; your own reputation, so carefully tended, could suffer by association with my decision. And yet, I believe that together, we might endure it all. Ireland is changing, even in its strife, and perhaps we could find a quiet corner of it where we might build a life, simple, honest, and full of love.

Before I take any step, however, I must know your heart. Do you feel as I do? Does the thought of a shared life fill you with as much hope and joy as it does me? I ask not out of selfishness but in earnest; I cannot bear to act if it would bring you pain.

Please, if you can, write to me. Be honest, even if it should wound me. I will abide by your will, for my love for you is as much about your happiness as my own.

Yours in faith, in love, and in hope,

Leo.

❧ ❧ ❧ ❧

Coleman explained to his Sergeant the situation surrounding the child that was Alice Duffy's.

"What do you want to do?" he asked.

"I would like you to accompany me to the parochial house and question Father Michael."

"Very well," the Sergeant said.

❧ ❧ ❧ ❧

Jimmy and Alice sat on a bench in a park and watched their son with this stranger. "This must be someone the couple that adopted him have employed to take him on outings," Alice said. "She is quite young, 20 years old maybe. She doesn't have any motherly instincts. She is calling our son Zach. He seems happy, doesn't he?" Jimmy said. Alice just wanted to go and grab him right now.

But Kathleen had talked sense. She had got the names and address of the couple and before handing it over, she asked them to please think about any intervention with them.

They talked about little else, only getting him back. But they couldn't come up with a solution.

Jimmy said to Alice. "If one of us was to become friends with the girl that is with our son, we could maybe learn a bit about her and if there was a time when we could get James off her."

Jimmy felt this was a very rough plan, but it was all he could think of.

They watched them leave the park and started back to Kathleen's home.

"We will speak to Kathleen and her mother about that," Alice said.

❧ ❧ ❧ ❧

The farm manager was back, and the price was agreed.

"This will be good," Pete said to his son Connor.

"People will see the tractor working as opposed to being sat here. If they see how quickly a field can be prepared for a crop the demand will increase."

Connor saw the excitement in his father and was overjoyed.

He was on his way to the address about the enquiry for the Austin 20 that day. He knocked the big brass knob on the door and was greeted by a servant.

"I heard about an enquiry for a motor car," Connor said.

"This is the bishop's residence," the servant answered.

Connor looked and waited for the girl to say something else.

"Wait there," she eventually said.

"Bring him," he heard from inside.

Connor was shown into a beautiful room full of polished furniture and shining candle holders.

"Good morning, Mr Flaherty," the bishop bellowed from a big chair behind a large desk.

"Good morning to you, too," Connor replied.

"Now, this motor."

"Yes," Connor started. "I have been to the factory in Birmingham and can get it for you early next year."

"Have you seen the car?"

"Yes. It's an impressive motor car for sure. It will cost in the region of nine hundred pounds by the time it is delivered to your door."

"Have you someone who knows how it works?" the bishop asked.

"You will learn quite quickly," Connor said.

"Oh no my boy, I want someone to look after all that. I couldn't possibly have time for all that.

My fellow bishops have a man that does all of that."

Well, aren't you something, Connor thought.

"Yes," Connor said. "What will this man be paid for this?" he asked.

"Well now," the bishop said. "He would live in and wear a uniform. He would have the motor car ready at all times. He will address me as Your Grace and only speak when spoken to.

For that my boy he will earn thirty pounds a year."

"Will you pay a deposit today, Your Grace?" Connor asked.

"Yes, my boy."

✖ ✖ ✖ ✖

Sarah read the letter from Leo again.

What an idiot she was! We were friends, she said looking at the words written.

You are in the clergy. How did she not see this coming? 'I must write back but I don't know what to say.'

She eventually wrote:

Dear Leo

I hope this letter finds you well. I want to thank you for your kind words and for the courage it must have taken to share your thoughts and feelings with me. It is not easy to be so open, and I deeply respect your honesty and sincerity.

You are a man of great integrity and compassion, and I have always valued our friendship. However, I must be truthful in return, as you deserve nothing less. While I hold you in the highest regard, my feelings for you have always been those of a dear friend and nothing more.

I am also compelled to tell you that my heart has been promised elsewhere. This does not diminish the care and respect I feel for you, but I cannot give you the love you seek. I am sorry if my words or actions ever gave you reason to think otherwise. It was never my intention to cause you hurt or confusion.

Your decision to reconsider your path in the Church is a deeply personal one, and I would not presume to advise you on such a weighty matter. However, I hope that whatever choice you make, it will be guided by reflection and peace rather than the pain of this moment. You have a calling that brings comfort and light to so many, and I believe your gifts are a blessing to those you serve.

Please know that I am here as a friend if you need someone to talk to during this time. I wish you strength and clarity as you navigate this chapter of your life.

With every kindness,

Sarah.

∾ ∾ ∾ ∾

Father Michael was livid.

How dare he! After all he had done for him. He would renounce him from the altar. The door knocked. He would punch him again he decided. He got up and opened the door quickly to see the two uniformed RIC men standing there.

"Father Michael. Can we have a word?" the Sergeant said.

"Yes, yes. Come on in. Take a seat, won't you?"

"Let's get straight to it," the Sergeant started. "You removed the child of Alice Flaherty from Bohermore and that child is in a place unknown to us. We wish to see the consent documents for that removal."

Father Michael looked at the two men for a long moment. He was considering refusing them but to what end?

"This is very unusual," he eventually said. "We do God's work here; we uphold the moral teachings laid down by the faith."

"I understand," the Sergeant said, "we are just her to make sure everything was done correctly as I'm sure a man of the cloth will appreciate."

"Of course. I have everything here."

He reached for the keys and unlocked the drawer. He lifted the documents out before him on his desk.

"I have her signed consent here."

He was about to hand a sheet of paper to the Sergeant when he saw that it was not the consent document, he expected it to be.

"I don't appear to have it as I thought I did," he said in a flustered voice.

"Can you try a bit harder to locate it?" Coleman spoke for the first time.

After he had rummaged through the drawer for another minute or so he said, "It's not here. Possibly it is in Bohermore."

The Sergeant and Coleman had expected this, and the Sergeant told him sternly that if consent is not presented then, "We will insist that the child be returned to its mother. I have it on firm authority, Father Michael, that such consent was not obtained. We will wait for you to resolve this serious matter as soon as possible." They bade him good day and left.

Father Michael immediately started writing a letter.

"Your Grace,

I write to you with a matter of great delicacy and urgency, seeking your guidance and wisdom. It has come to light that a child (Master James Flaherty) from this parish was placed with a family under your jurisdiction in America without the proper consent of the child's mother. This situation has caused considerable distress, and the local authorities here in Ireland are now involved.

The mother of the child, who had been led to believe her child was being cared for temporarily, has recently discovered the arrangement and is seeking the return of her child. The Royal Irish Constabulary has approached me, as the local parish priest, to assist in facilitating the return of the child. They insist that, given the circumstances, the mother's rights must be respected, and they are prepared to pursue the matter formally if necessary.

The family with whom you placed the child, to my knowledge, is entirely unaware of these irregularities and is acting in good faith. However, the fact remains that consent was not obtained, and this matter weighs heavily on my conscience.

I seek your guidance on how we might address this situation. Specifically:

1. How should we communicate with the family to explain the need for the child's return without causing undue distress?

2. Are there legal or procedural measures in America we must undertake to facilitate the child's return?

3. How might we assist the mother here in Ireland to reconcile the events and the pain she has endured?

This situation is most regrettable, and I humbly admit that better oversight and caution on my part could have prevented it. I am prepared to do all in my power to rectify this and to ensure such an occurrence does not happen again.

I await your advice on how best to proceed and assure you of my prayers as we navigate this difficult matter.

Yours faithfully in Christ,

Father Michael.

My curate, Father Michael thought.

He removed the drawer and had a closer look at the contents. The money is all here. The consent form is all that is missing. This letter from Bohermore. How did that get here? What is happening here?

❧ ❧ ❧ ❧

Leo had received the letter from Sarah.

He read it only once. His mind was in a quandary. He had waited to hear from Sarah before deciding about whether to go as directed to Lough Derg. Now, that was the last place he wanted to be.

Then a little pathway had opened up in his brain. He was encouraged to walk down the path. People called to him, where are you going, come back, but he didn't care about them. His mother called, don't go son, but he ignored her too, we were friends he heard Sarah call, he ignored her.

He went to the turf shed and took what he needed. He walked down through the small fields. The path was leading him there. He climbed up and tied a secure knot to the branch and placed the other end around his neck. Before he stepped off the branch he said, "I'm at peace now."

≈ ≈ ≈ ≈

Connor asked Pat if he was interested in the position at the bishop's residence.

"I will be delighted," he replied.

"You must get into the way of turning yourself out better," Connor said in as nice a way as he could muster.

"I will clean myself for the pleasure of driving that motor car," he said smiling.

Alice and Jimmy were suggesting to Kathleen about befriending the girl that looked after James. She agreed to try.

Today they are waiting in the park. Kathleen sat on a different bench and watched the girl walk along with the child. Kathleen got up and walked towards them. "Hi," Kathleen said. "Isn't it a lovely day for a walk? What's your baby's name? Oh, it's Zach," she said. "I'm his nanny."

"I'm Kathleen," and she offered her hand. "An Irish name, I'm Maureen," she said, "I'm from County Longford in Ireland." "My mother is from Mayo," Kathleen said in a cheery voice.

"I work in a big house as a domestic," she went on.

"There are no children thank goodness. I have enough to be doing without looking after little ones.

Do you have many to mind?"

"Just Zach," she replied.

"Do you live in?" Kathleen asked.

"Yes," Maureen replied.

"He will be starting school now and I will have more time for other things. I don't get to go anywhere or see people. They keep giving me lots to do."

"I'm the same," Kathleen told her. "I have to cook, wash, clean the big house and if guests call let them in and make tea. The people I work for go away on trips so I have freedom then. But I make sure the house is spotless when they return."

"My ones both work, he has a business and she is clerk or something at the bank. They visit his mother, but I have to go with them. Hopefully they will soon be going to Newport, Rhode Island.

They have a summer house there. Last time they went Zach nearly got drowned. There are loads of water things to do. They have a boat, and she wasn't watching him while I had been sent to fetch them drinks.

"I was lucky because I wanted Zach to come and get the drinks with me, but she said to leave him. So, I couldn't be blamed.

"They like to go to elegant garden parties and meet people like themselves. But they might not take me along this time because of what happened."

"Will Zach go with them?" Kathleen asked.

"I hope so. If he does, I am going to go dancing."

"Can I come too?"

"Yes. Wouldn't that be fun?"

∾ ∾ ∾ ∾

Father Michael decided he would punish sister Tessa.

He wrote:

To the Most Reverend Mother Superior, Bohermore.

Reverend Mother,

I write to you in regard to a matter of some concern involving Sister Tessa, whose recent behaviour I must bring to your attention. It pains me to report that her conduct during our recent interactions has shown a troubling lack of respect for her vows of obedience and the authority vested in the clergy.

Whilst doing God's work, Sister Tessa displayed an attitude that I can only describe as defiant. She failed to get written consent from Alice

Flaherty for the safe placement of her child. She questioned my decision regarding parish matters in a manner that was neither appropriate nor in keeping with her sacred calling. Such actions, if left unchecked, risk undermining not only the harmony of your community but also the broader mission of the Church.

As her superior, I ask that you address this matter with the seriousness it warrants. A firm reprimand, emphasising the importance of humility, obedience, and respect for ecclesiastical authority, is, in my view, necessary to correct her course. Additionally, it may be beneficial for her to undertake a period of reflection and spiritual penance to realign herself with the values and responsibilities of her vocation.

I trust in your wisdom to handle this matter in a manner befitting the dignity of your position and the good of your community. Please do not hesitate to reach out should you require further details or wish to discuss this matter further.

May God bless you in your leadership and grant you strength in guiding your sisters in Christ.

Yours in Christ,

Father Michael.

ৡ ৡ ৡ ৡ

Mol was sitting with party colleagues on January 21st 1919. They were discussing the ambush in County Tipperary that had just taken place. Irish Volunteers had ambushed a convoy of Royal Irish Constabulary officers.

Mol had been finding as much as she could about David Lloyd George, the British Prime Minister.

"We can expect a big response," she said.

ৡ ৡ ৡ ৡ

Connor was chatting to his father. "Things have started to slow down," he said. "The Spanish Flu is having devastating effects on labour."

Pete said Mol had told him about the Land Reforms where 'our farmers would get more land', this could help with the farm machinery side.

Connor said, "You are a genius. We will build that side of things and leave the motor cars until we see a call for them."

The bishop in Boston had read Father Michael's letter.

What an imbecile! He thought. Time will resolve the matter, he decided. I will draw it out and it will most likely go away.

Dear Father Michael,

I have received your letter regarding the return of the child to Ireland, and I am deeply concerned by the situation you have outlined. The matter of consent, or rather the lack thereof, from the child's mother is a significant issue that cannot be overlooked.

As you know, the protection and well-being of children must be at the forefront of all decisions, and we must always act in accordance with both civil law and our religious principles. While I understand the circumstances in which this child was placed with a family in America, the absence of consent from the child's mother raises serious moral and legal concerns. The child must, of course, be returned to the care of the mother unless she is deemed unfit to provide care, in which case further action would be necessary.

In light of this, I must advise that you make arrangements for the child's safe return to Ireland as soon as possible. This must be done in a way that ensures the child's best interests are safeguarded, and that the mother's rights are respected. Should there be any further complications regarding the welfare of the child or the mother's ability to care for them, I recommend that you consult with local authorities or social services in Ireland to determine the best course of action.

I understand that this may not be the outcome you hoped for, but it is crucial that we uphold the integrity of our actions, particularly when it comes to matters involving the care and custody of children. We must always ensure that consent, transparency, and the law are respected in all such cases.

Please keep me updated on your progress, and should you need any further guidance or assistance, do not hesitate to contact me.

May God grant you wisdom and strength as you navigate this difficult situation.

Yours in Christ,

⇛⇛⇛⇛

Leo's lifeless body was taken down by two neighbours that found him. It appeared to them that he had been there for several days. They laid him on the ground and walked towards his home. It was early Sunday morning and people were getting ready for mass. The men broke the news to Leo's parents and word spread quickly around the parish. A neighbour was sent to fetch the priest to give the last rites.

Father Michael was in the sacristy and dismissed the tap on the door. He commenced mass and was evidently prepared for his carefully written sermon.

"Dear Brothers and Sisters in Christ,

Today, I find it necessary to speak frankly and openly about a matter that weighs heavily upon my heart. As your priest, it is my duty to guide not only your spiritual lives but to also ensure the integrity of the mission we share in service to God. In our community, the bond between the priest and his curate is one of mutual respect and trust, as we work together to uphold the values of Christ's teachings. However, there are moments when this bond must be addressed, especially when it is compromised by actions that undermine our collective duty.

"It has come to my attention, and I believe it must be addressed publicly, that one of my curates has, through his actions, failed to live up to the responsibilities entrusted to him. His conduct has at times been more fitting for a silly child than a priest dedicated to the service of God and the good of His people. This, my dear friends, is a matter of great concern.

"We must remember, as clergy, that we are held to a higher standard. Our behaviour must reflect the gravity of the office we hold. We are not here to indulge in childish whims or to carry on with the carefree abandon of youth. Our lives are dedicated to the service of the Lord and His people, and we are called to act with wisdom, maturity, and above all, with a sense of responsibility. To do otherwise is to dishonour the calling we have received and to mislead those who look to us for guidance.

"We must ask ourselves: are we behaving in a way that builds up the Kingdom of God, or are we engaging in actions that detract from the seriousness of our ministry? Are we, as priests, embodying the dignity and respect that comes with our role, or are we allowing foolishness to creep in, as though we have not yet understood the weight of our vows?

"Let me be clear, this is not a matter of anger, but of concern. The curate in question is, in many ways, a good man with much potential. But we cannot afford to allow personal immaturity or thoughtless actions to overshadow the gravity of the vocation we share. The work of the Church requires serious dedication, self-discipline, and a commitment to the well-being of our congregation.

"I call upon my curate, and indeed, all of us, to reflect on our conduct. Let us not be like children who act without thought, but instead, let us be mature stewards of the grace and responsibility given to us. Let us live our lives as examples of integrity, wisdom, and reverence for the sacred trust we hold.

"I ask for your prayers, that all of us, especially those of us in the clergy, may be filled with the wisdom and fortitude to carry out our duties with the seriousness and commitment that they demand.

"May God guide us in all that we do, and may He grant us the humility to learn from our mistakes and the courage to grow in His service.

Amen."

A murmur of whispers could be heard throughout the congregation.

People looked at Father Michael with disdain on their faces. They had loved the young curate. He was only starting out and they felt he was one of them.

Sarah heard the news. Her mother had been at mass. She couldn't tell her what Father Michael had said in his sermon. She couldn't believe that he would ever do such a thing. He was always so happy and funny. Life is very difficult she thought. She then wondered if Leo had told people about his change of heart with his devotion to the church. Did he tell people that he had fallen in love with her? People could blame her.

She convinced herself through her tears that she didn't lead him to believe it was any more than friendship. She remembered teasing him about bringing her to America with him. That was her mistake she started to believe.

≈ ≈ ≈ ≈

Pat was in Dublin. He was there to collect the new Austin motor car. When he got off the train at Kingsbridge he noticed there was a large presence of men in military uniform. He walked through the city and was aware of the heightened tensions.

He arrived at the depot and introduced himself to a gentleman who checked the details about the motor car.

"Yes, sir. Follow me." Pat was very excited.

He was shown how to use the starter handle, the window wipers, the lights, the horn and the heater.

He set off on his journey to the West. He waved at people that stood out to watch the big motor car drive past.

Connor had given Pat a map so that he could work out how to get to Galway. He marked out three towns, Kinnegad, Athlone and Ballinasloe. He had difficulty getting past carts so far and he hadn't seen any sign of Kinnegad yet. Some stretches of the road were quite good and the motor car ran smoothly but other parts had him worried that he would break something. Deep potholes and muddy parts made the motor car struggle.

So far, he had been driving for eight hours and he was only in Ballinasloe. The roads had become more dangerous now with light fading and the road difficult to see even with the lights. Eventually he arrived no less than twelve hours from when he has set off.

Connor and his father were waiting for him and were shocked at the sight of the car. It was far from looking like a new motor car. They got buckets of water and proceeded to clean it. They decided they would have it in the yard for a couple of days so that people could see it.

Kathleen and Maureen were going to a dance. The couple had gone on a short vacation and taken Zach with them.

The dance hall was in south Boston and was one that would be overseen by clergy, Kathleen had told Maureen. "Have you a modest dress?" she asked, "they won't let you in otherwise."

Jimmy and Alice went too.

Kathleen had suggested it. "Meet Maureen by chance and talk to her about Ireland. If ye see her in the park after that at least ye will get to be a bit closer to your son."

They liked that plan.

Kathleen told Jimmy that he needed a suit.

"I will see what his nibs has in his vast wardrobe. He is fat," she laughed, "but he might have something from when he was a bit smaller."

Kathleen was the odd one out. Maureen, Jimmy and Alice were used to set dancing, jigs and reels. Kathleen was in awe of their seemingly natural ability.

With sweat lashing off them, Alice and Jimmy stood close to Maureen and Kathleen. "It's great music," Jimmy said. "It is the best fun," Maureen said. They introduced each other's names, and they fell into talking about home.

Tessa was summoned to the Mother Superior's office. She stood and waited to be addressed.

"Sister, there are accusations of insubordination made against you by Father Michael. Can you explain yourself?"

"I'm sorry, Mother," she started. "He was very aggressive when he came asking for a mother's signed consent form. I told him we didn't have the mother's consent. He demanded something that she had signed and the only thing we had was in the marriage registry book."

"Go on," the Mother Superior said.

"Well, I gave it to him and he left. But before he did, I put a hand written note to say consent had not been signed by Alice Flaherty mother of James Flaherty."

"Well, sister. He wants me to punish you as severely as possible. However, I don't see that you did anything wrong. We made the mistake of letting him take the child in the first place.

"I will be placing you in charge of gaining written consent where the mother is adamant that she wants to forego her right to the child and maintaining that record in a logbook that we will maintain from this day on.

"Should Father Michael turn up at this door again you are to fetch me.

"Now go back to your duties sister."

કે કે કે કે

At Leo's wake a group of parishioners led by Kate Flaherty were in a back room.

Kate had written a letter which they had discussed following Father Michael's sermon.

The letter was going to be sent to the bishop.

She read it out to them:

Your Excellency,

We, the undersigned parishioners of Clifton Parish, write to you with heavy hearts and a deep sense of duty regarding the conduct and demeanour of our current parish priest, Father Michael. It is with the utmost respect for your office and for the Church that we feel compelled to bring this matter to your attention, as it directly affects the spiritual well-being of our parish community.

While we acknowledge the burden of leadership and the imperfections inherent in all human beings, we must express our profound disappointment and distress regarding Father Michael's behaviour and approach to his congregation. Over time, we have observed a pattern of unfeeling and belligerent conduct that has caused hurt and alienation among many of our parishioners.

Among the specific concerns we wish to highlight are the following:

1. Lack of pastoral care

Father Michael has repeatedly displayed a lack of compassion and understanding when dealing with the personal and spiritual needs of parishioners. Those seeking counsel or comfort in times of difficulty often feel dismissed or judged, rather than embraced with the love and care that should characterise a shepherd of Christ's flock.

2. Harsh and belligerent tone

His manner during homilies and in personal interactions is frequently harsh, critical, and lacking in the gentleness that draws people closer to the faith. Many feel more discouraged than inspired by his words, which often come across as scolding rather than guiding.

3. Division within the community

Father Michael's approach has fostered division rather than unity within the parish. Several longstanding parishioners have withdrawn from active participation in church life, citing his attitude and behaviour as a significant factor.

We believe that the role of a parish priest is not only to teach and lead but also to inspire and nurture the faith of the people in his care. Sadly, under Father Michael's leadership, many of us feel spiritually adrift and unwelcome in our own parish.

It is with great humility and respect that we ask Your Excellency to consider assigning a new priest to our parish, someone whose leadership style is more reflective of the compassionate example set by Our Lord Jesus Christ. We trust in your wisdom and judgment to take the necessary steps to restore peace and harmony within our community.

We pray for Father Michael, that he may find the grace and guidance he needs to fulfil his vocation in a manner that reflects Christ's love. We also pray for you, that you may have the strength to make decisions that serve the greater good of your parish.

With faith and hope,

Names and contact information, if required.

ﻋ ﻋ ﻋ ﻋ

Father Michael arrived at the bishop's residence. He didn't have an appointment but needed his guidance. While he was waiting, he heard the engine of a motor car pull up and he stood up to look out the window.

Pat Flaherty, well I never, he muttered. What is he doing here of all places?

Then he was more surprised to see His Grace approach him and shake his hand. Pat looked very smart and was being very polite. They were walking around the motor car. Was he admiring Pat's motor car? They walked away together towards one of the many buildings connecting the bishop's courtyard.

After a long wait he was told by a servant that the bishop would see him now.

"Well now, Father Michael. Where do we start?"

"What's he doing here?" he interrupted.

"What?"

"That man with the car."

"Shut up and listen," he said. "I received a letter from the bishop's palace in Boston.

Another from the Mother Superior in Bohermore and yet another from the parishioners of your parish.

Your curate ended his own life. What am I to do with you? I am considering a parish on the islands. Father Louis is elderly and needs help. He struggles to go around the three islands. As soon as I find a suitable replacement that is what I will do, I have decided.

"Regarding the child you removed from Bohermore. I am lost for words. You informed me that the paperwork was in order but it's clearly not. Now, in Bohermore, I'm informed you acted like a playground bully to the nuns. The Mother Superior says she will not permit you near the building again.

"Your curate ended his own life. He had recently been beaten and had to be in hospital for several weeks. Was this your doing?"

The bishop raised his hand, "Don't speak, I'm not finished yet. And today, I received a letter from your own parishioners requesting you be moved from the parish. Now what do you wish to say?"

"I will happily accept my reassignment Your Grace."

୬ ୬ ୬ ୬

Alice and Maureen had arranged to meet in the park after the success of the dance.

Alice knew James wouldn't be with her because the family was still on vacation.

When Maureen turned up, they decided to walk and chat. Maureen loved talking about home and Alice felt guilty about deceiving her.

"Stop Maureen," she said. "I cannot lie to you."

Maureen said, "What are you saying?"

"I haven't been honest with you, and I cannot lie. Will you listen until I tell you and then you can tell me to get lost?"

Maureen was a bit scared but said, "OK."

Alice started with the love affair with Jimmy and then his disappearance. Then her heartbreak believing he had abandoned her. Then the fight with Pat. And on she went with the whole story.

"And that is why Jimmy and myself are here," she said.

Maureen looked at Alice with tears in her eyes. "Are you telling me the truth?"

"I told you I couldn't lie."

"But that is the worst thing I have ever heard."

"You are a young girl," Alice said. "I don't expect you to know what we can do, but at least now you know the truth."

❧ ❧ ❧ ❧

Father Michael was furious. He came out of the bishop's house and got the handle to start the car.

He turned the handle with such fury that he snapped the end piece that slots into the crankshaft.

He fired the handle away. When he went to retrieve it, he saw Pat. He was washing the motor car in the bishop's courtyard.

"Can you give me a hand with my motor car?" he asked.

"I would like to Father, but I have this to do for His Grace, you see."

Father Michael looked at him long and hard. He threw the handle into the motor car and started walking. How was he in a worse position than that Pat Flaherty was? There he is with fancy clothes on and washing the big car. How did he get into this mess? He told himself he could have explained away each of the charges the bishop put to him but, when they were all together, he didn't even try. What was the point?

❧ ❧ ❧ ❧

Connor hadn't seen Sarah since Leo's funeral. She was feeling very hurt by the whole situation.

He told her it couldn't be her fault, but she felt it was. She had told nobody about the letter but today when Connor came, she would tell him.

They cycled to the beach and started to walk. "Will you read what Leo sent to me?" she asked.

He took the letter and carefully read it. After he finished, he folded it and put his arms around her.

"It's not your fault," he said. "How could you have known? If I was in your shoes, I would plainly say good bye to Leo by destroying that letter. While you have it, you will have the guilt. We've all had a crush on someone especially when we were in school," he went on. "It's all part of living and growing as a person. You were possibly his childish crush and because he had tied himself to his faith, he must have been unable to cope. Do you think he had really thought about how the two of you could have been together? Did he ever tell you what happened to him when he had to go hospital that time?"

"Yes, he did. Father Michael punched him, and he fell down. That's all he could remember."

"Father Michael," Connor said.

"Wouldn't you know?"

"Well, that makes sense," Connor started. "Leo felt rejected by his first love which is what he chose when he went into the priesthood. He turned to someone who showed him kindness. Had he been able to say all he said in the letter to your face it could have been different. You weren't to know how venerable he was. Put the letter into the water and let the tide take it away. Say your final goodbye."

She put her arms around him now and he held her close.

"We will do it together," she suggested.

They watched as it ebbed and flowed with the gentle waves of a tide on the turn.

Maureen and Alice continued to walk side by side.

"I have something I want to tell you now". Maureen said. "I have been afraid to tell anyone. He has tried to make me do it with him." Alice had an enquiring look on her face. "Him. Zach's adoptive father. When I pulled away, he tried to force me. Then he'd say he was sorry and all that. I hate him."

Alice put her arms around her and held her close.

"Some men are worse than animals," she said.

"You need to start looking for work somewhere else."

"It's not that easy. You will need a letter when you leave. He wouldn't give me one."

"You didn't have a letter when you started, did you?" Alice asked.

"No, but a lot of these people know each other."

"Would you tell Kathleen what you told me, because she is the cleverest girl I ever met for someone so young in years."

"I will tell her if she promises not to say to anyone."

૭ ૭ ૭ ૭

Eve and Coleman were sitting in the Flaherty kitchen. They were there at Mol's request. Connor, Pete and Kate were already there. Mol came from the parlour where she worked when she wasn't in Dublin.

"Hello," she said as she sat down.

"Coleman, you may know much of what we are here to discuss so if you are permitted please add any detail I miss. The British have assembled a force called the "Black and Tans". They have been formed to bolster the RIC, which they believe are struggling to control the increasing attacks against the British. Recruits are primarily ex-soldiers from Britain, many of whom have served in The Great War and were struggling to reintegrate into civilian life. Many of these men fought alongside Irish men in the war.

"New recruits are currently being rushed through training and as a result are badly disciplined. These men know nothing about Ireland or the political landscape."

"Why are they called that?" Eve asked Mol.

"It's more of a nickname," Mol said, "it comes from their uniforms, a mix of dark green RIC tunics and khaki military trousers, it resembles the colours of a pack of foxhounds. Recently there was a RIC member shot in Balbriggan, the resulting backlash was severe. Random shootings, businesses burned and homes pulled asunder. There are no rules that we can see. They do what they feel like. This is not to be taken lightly. They will stop at nothing."

Coleman said, "We are lucky in our remoteness here. But if attention is drawn to an area, they will arrive in force. Travel to and from Dublin and Cork is dangerous right now."

Mol said, "What we speak of here today must stay between us. This gathering would see all of us executed in an instant. The British presence in Ireland is close to an end. Believe me. They won't be able to contain the rise of the Irish people. Trying to beat us into submission won't work. Make friends, Coleman, if you intend to continue living here."

Eve knew what Mol meant but wanted her to say more so that Coleman would understand fully the danger ahead. "What do you mean Mol?" she said.

"What I mean is simply protect those around you. Steer trouble away. Be seen to be someone who cares about the people here. Right now, the RIC being flanked by this new plague of Black and Tans are hated the country over. Don't be one that is hated.

"We haven't heard from Jimmy and Alice. They will get a shock when they come home. Cork is a particularly dangerous place right now."

Pete asked, "Is there anything we can do to stay on their right side?"

"Get rid of anything you have that could be viewed as being anti British. Have a pleasant manner, have alcohol and tobacco to offer for the great work they are doing and importantly, keep women and children out of sight. Avoid any gatherings of any kind. Even attending mass is dangerous because they are well aware that there are many in the Church that support the cause especially some priests."

༉ ༉ ༉ ༉

Pat was fed up. All he did was wait to be told to get the motor car ready. It was ready all the time, but they rarely went anywhere. The servant girl Treasa was a miserable cow, he thought. She seemed to think he was a nobody.

He took his meals in the back kitchen in silence. She wasn't happy about having to feed him.

"Wipe your feet before you come in here," was her favourite scowl at him.

Today Treasa was ironing vestments while Pat ate away at a bowl of soup. It was full of chicken bones but tasty all the same. "You have a lot to do" he thought, to try and get a bit of conversation out of her.

"Too bloody much," she replied. "That Father Michael isn't very nice, is he?"

Pat went on. "Well not to me anyway."

"He is a strange one for sure," she said. "He thinks he is above everyone. I don't give him any time at all. He got a good kick in the arse though. He is moving away off out to the islands."

"Bloody serves him right."

She was talking freely now.

"The auld priest on the islands is near dead and isn't able to do hardly anything so he is taking over from him. The islanders are hardy people."

"Have you been there?" he asked her to keep the flow of conversation going.

"Yes, a few times, we have an uncle on Inis Meáin. Father Michael will have to accept that the people there are supportive of the Republican cause, the majority of the islanders favour Sinn Féin and the fight for

Irish independence. It is well known that they occasionally assist the cause by providing food, shelter and safe passage for individuals fleeing British."

"Where are his loyalties?" Pat asked.

"He doesn't have any," she replied. "Only to himself."

❧ ❧ ❧ ❧

Jimmy had been to the port and had checked the boat timetables. He missed home and was desperate to get the three of them onto the boat home. He enquired about casual work at the port but was told that there were many people that turned up every day looking for the same.

He stood looking at an automobile station and missed the simplicity of Connor's place at home. He walked into a workshop area and started chatting to a man in oily clothing.

"Fine motor cars," Jimmy said.

"Sure are, when they don't breakdown," the man replied.

"I have worked on the Model T," Jimmy informed him.

"Well, they are all the same really," he insisted. "Just a bit trickier at times. What are you doing, are you waiting for someone off the ship?"

"Not at all," Jimmy said. "I'm thinking about a bit of casual kind of work."

"Would you come back tomorrow?" he asked. "There might be something here since you have done it before."

"By God, I will for sure," Jimmy said.

He left with a spring in his step.

❧ ❧ ❧ ❧

Kathleen met Maureen in the park and sat recalling the dance. "Can we go again?" Maureen asked excitedly.

"Why wouldn't we?"

"When suits you?"

"I will have to see," Maureen said.

"You are not happy in that place," Kathleen said. "Alice told me."

"I have got a bit used to it now, I kinda know how to handle him. When the wife leaves, I make sure Zach is with me all the time. But he is cunning, he will do his best to get me to do something away from Zach, and then he follows me. They are back today."

"Can you come here tomorrow?" Kathleen asked.

"Yes, I come every day."

"Ok. Alice and Jimmy will be here."

∾ ∾ ∾ ∾

Pat decided to try and meet his old Sergeant from the RIC station. He recalled the excitement when he had provided the information to Chamberlain. He could try to meet him away from the station so that nobody would know. He decided that a visit to his home would be the easiest.

He thought he would love to be involved in something exciting again. He decided to strike while the iron was hot. He asked Treasa to see if the bishop was free. He told her, "We wanted to get a fill up of gasoline."

The bishop said, "My boy, you don't have to bother me with such things. Just do it."

He left at the same time he knew the Sergeant left the station. He took the bishop's motor car along the narrow road to the Sergeant's house and arrived as the Sergeant was cycling the last hundred yards home. He tooted the horn, and the Sergeant looked at him crossly.

"How do you do, Sergeant?" Pat said. The Sergeant was flabbergasted to see him driving the big car.

"Well, if it isn't Pat Flaherty," he said getting off the bicycle.

"Ah," said Pat. "I look after the car for His Grace the bishop. Sure, it's a grand handy job for me."

"And what do you want here may I ask?"

"Well, I have news that might be of interest to you."

"Oh, have you indeed?"

"Yes," Pat said.

"And how might you have come on this news may I ask?"

"No indeed you may not. I just hear things."

"Well, what is it then?"

"Before I tell you, I need something of my own," Pat said.

"And what would that be then?"

"I want my job with the RIC back, but I will be continuing in my job but letting you know of any trouble coming your way. You see I drive the bishop to all the fancy church services and I stay around outside with the drivers of the cars for all the other people that can afford to own a motor car. They talk, and I listen. Do we have an agreement, Sergeant?" Pat asked.

"Well now, I will have to speak to my superiors," the Sergeant replied.

"Very well," Pat said and got into the car. The Sergeant said, "Don't come here again. I will find you. Do you hear that?" "Yes," Pat said.

Pat drove back down the narrow road and thought, now Pat, that is using your head.

❧ ❧ ❧ ❧

Jimmy returned to the automobile garage and was met by the man he spoke to the previous day.

"Gus is my name," he said as he held out his hand. "You can help me here. You will earn one dollar per hour, and I usually work 48 hours a week. Would that make you happy?" he asked. Jimmy shook his hand again warmly.

"When can you start?" Gus asked.

"Now," Jimmy said.

"That's what I was hoping you would say."

They started working on replacing a broken windscreen followed by replacing a tyre. There were so many things to do that he forgot about time.

₭₭₭₭

The Sergeant had a bit of a dilemma. Should he let what Pat had said go or should he speak to his superiors about it? 'Things have been quiet here for a long time, ever since the atrocious attack that night. And Pat was involved in that too,' he recalled.

If there was trouble planned and was coming his way, he would be better off to be prepared. However, he liked the people here. They were good honest hardworking people. Could he bring the ruthless Black and Tans to their doors? Better to be safe than sorry, he decided. He telephoned his superior and explained the situation.

"He was onboarded by Chamberlain initially, you say, and he delivered news of the arms shipment that was intercepted, you say?" "Yes sir," the Sergeant said.

"It's an absolute must to have him on board.'

The Sergeant now felt he had made the correct decision. He couldn't face the journey to the bishop's residence, instead decided to think.

Taking one of the two cars that had been rarely used would be dangerous and in any case, he would be quicker by bicycle.

₭₭₭₭

Connor and his father had considered modifying horse drawn machinery to be used with tractors. This was a problem they were having with the sale of new tractors. The men buying the tractor were stretching their resources to the limit and the prospect of having to purchase any or all the implements was just not possible.

They were looking at opening up the forge that had been there originally. It seemed to be a good plan.

The two men sat down and worked on the fact that metals were heated in the forge until they became malleable and then hammered together to form a bond. This method they knew was used by blacksmiths over the years.

"I don't want you having to do that work," Connor said to his father.

"Sure, what else would I be at," he replied. "Sure, aren't I happy to be at something. I am looking forward to seeing if it works."

ഇ ഇ ഇ ഇ

The Sergeant needed a plan to be able to get the information from Pat without having to travel all that way and to be able to remain inconspicuous. He had no dealings with Pat's brother Connor at the car garage, but the RIC did have two cars and Pat drove the car for the bishop. No, he decided against that.

He needed to speak to him anyway to get the information he had so he would go to where he worked out of uniform for safety. He would go first thing in the morning, he decided.

ഇ ഇ ഇ ഇ

Mol was never so tired. She hadn't seen Joe in months. She was nearly constantly in Dublin.

The Brotherhood was now referred to as the Irish Republican Army (IRA). They were targeting British forces, particularly the RIC through ambushes and assassinations.

The British government were responding by deploying paramilitary forces like the Black and Tans and the Auxiliary Division, who became notorious for their brutality.

On the morning of November 21st 1920, the IRA assassinated 14 British intelligence agents known as the Cairo Gang, in Dublin.

That afternoon, British forces retaliated by firing into the crowd at Croke Park during a Gaelic football match. The match was part of a Gaelic Athletic Association challenge game between Dublin and Tipperary and was attended by over 5,000 people.

Mol was one of a group that organised the game.

It was a fundraising effort for the Irish Republican Prisoners' Dependents Fund, organised to support the families of imprisoned IRA members.

British forces, including the Auxiliary Division and the RIC arrived at Croke Park during the match in response to the assassination earlier that morning.

Without warning, the British forces opened fire on the crowd, claiming they were searching for IRA members. 14 civilians were killed, including a player from Tipperary, Michael Hogan.

Mol and her colleagues were also looking into the fact that later that day, three IRA prisoners had been murdered in Dublin Castle under suspicious circumstances.

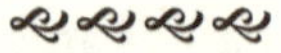

The Sergeant wheeled his bicycle the last bit of the journey.

Pat spotted him and took him into the car house.

"Ok," the Sergeant said. "You are with us, on advice from higher authority than me.

You will call at the RIC station to collect your pay, and you will leave a letter for my personal attention at the same time unless there is an urgent message. In that case you will use a telephone. I'm sure there is one here. You will telephone the station and ask to speak to myself only. It that understood?"

"Yes indeed," Pat replied.

"Now tell me what you have heard."

"There are insurgents being housed in Inis Meáin," Pat told him. "I heard they were involved in the killing of British forces in Cork recently. There is only a small number of people over there," he finished.

The Sergeant was about to say, "Is that all?" but decided instead to say,

"Very well."

Alice and Jimmy were in the park and saw Maureen and James come towards them. They both looked in awe at their child. He was dressed in beautiful clothes and his hair was neatly combed. James wanted to continue walking so they got up and walked as a group. Kathleen had said to be careful because anything they say could be repeated by the child unintentionally. Then the adoptive parents might get concerned.

James was completely unaware of who they were, and it hurt them both. They walked and chatted and eventually Alice saw an opportunity to lift him up close to her. It felt like heaven having her baby in her arms. She just wanted this moment to last forever.

Jimmy whispered quietly to Maureen about the possibility of taking him when the time was right.

"What am I to do then?" she said. "I would surely be put in jail for ever more."

"Would you consider coming with us?" he asked without having thought about it.

"I didn't think about that. I suppose I could go to more dances if I did," she said laughing.

"I will talk to Alice and Kathleen about that, and you have a think about it too," he said.

ৰ ৰ ৰ ৰ

The Sergeant summoned the Constables to the briefing room.

"We have insurgents in Inis Meáin," he said. "Our intelligence tells us they are being sheltered by the islanders."

This is what Coleman was dreading. The trouble was getting close.

"Anyone that has been to the islands will be aware that only the native tongue is spoken there. They are as hardy a people as there are on this earth. The landscape is harsh. They make their own soil by mixing sand and seaweed. Everybody knows everyone else. They won't talk to strangers. They certainly won't talk to us.

"So, this is what we will do. We watch the comings and goings. We gather intelligence on who is an islander and who is not. Anyone else is arrested and interrogated. Any questions?" he asked.

❧ ❧ ❧ ❧

Pete had the forge up and working.

He was studying a horse drawn plough. The long steel shaft that the horse would have pulled would be cut. The two arms the man held onto would also be cut. A second plough would be placed alongside so he could try and work out how they could become one.

"It won't be a masterpiece," he said to Connor.

"Would you be offended if I got an experienced man here to help us for a while?" Connor asked.

"Not at all son, sure I could learn from his ways."

"Old Tom's first cousin worked here in this very place," Connor said. "I remember the man," Pete said, "Seamus was his name."

"Yes, he is working up at the big house but doesn't get along with the manager. I could ask him," Connor said.

Connor went to the big house and heard the tractor engine.

He walked directly to where the engine was running but the tractor was stationary.

The farm manager was shouting at two farm hands. "You are ploughing too deep. That's why the wheel is spinning," he was saying.

"You bloody do it, so" one of the men said back.

Connor greeted the three men saying, "God bless the work."

The three men looked at him.

"Set the plough so that when you lower the lift arms it will have the plough pulled in a horizontal position.

If you hit a big stone or the single wheel is spinning, engage the differential lock."

"What was that you said?" the manager asked. "That made no sense."

"Did you read the book that came with it?"

"No. Should we have?"

"I'm looking for Seamus," Connor said.

"That's me," one of the men spoke.

"I have a need for some assistance with the old forge," he said. "If you would be willing to show my father how things are done, I could show this other gentleman how this is done."

"Deal," the manager said delighted.

~~~~

Kathleen, Jimmy and Alice were discussing the risks involved with simply running with James. Now the possibility of bringing Maureen with them.

Jesus, Kathleen said, "It's getting that twisted now that I think I might come too. And that is me adding a bit of humour to the madness. I'm not doing that. Right. Jimmy, tell us your end."

Jimmy said, "The ship will set off in daylight always. Late morning or early afternoon. They do that for safer navigation out of the port to sea. Boarding the ship is slow, they won't rush the passengers. I went and enquired about documentation for James but was told he will be fine without it due to his age. I asked if it was possible to get something as we were concerned about the ports in Europe. So, I have a travel pass now.

"I asked about our two adult tickets and child fare and was told James didn't need one. At this stage we were getting along great so I asked would our child be on the ship's inventory. Unlikely, I was told, but there is always a member of staff that can be a devil for details. I then asked can I purchase the tickets today and go whenever I felt like it. He started to get a bit uncomfortable at this stage, so I blamed you, Alice. He said you can purchase tickets easily and quickly whenever you are ready."

"Right," said Kathleen. "Now Alice, your side."
~~~~

"Once the couple leaves the house at around eight thirty in the morning, Maureen has Zach until around five thirty to six. Sometimes later. Maureen will have Zach in the lounge room when they get home, neither of them comes in to see him and he doesn't ask to see them either. Some nights she puts him to bed without ever seeing them."

Kathleen's mother who had been sitting quietly said, "That's shocking. Poor little lad."

Alice continued, "Towards the weekend, Thursday especially, they are nearly always home late.

If the ship leaves on Thursday next we will go."

❧ ❧ ❧ ❧

Coleman and Eve were walking along the beach.

"The trouble is coming near us," he told her. "They are watching the islands. We need to be careful."

"They come here for some produce," Eve said. "The people here cannot be asked not to sell to them, can they?"

"No," he said. "They will be watching for strangers amongst them."

"They are the loveliest, kindest people you know," Eve told him.

"Let Mol know what I told you, he said. "She will let her people know."

Eve was surprised. "Are you sure?"

"Yes," he said. "I want us to be able to live in peace when this is all over."

❧ ❧ ❧ ❧

Connor was explaining, "There are three arms connecting the plough to the tractor. The three arms are rigid. That means there has to be a way of getting the sock here at the front to glide horizontal through the ground. That is what this handle is for. You turn this to achieve that. I will show you now." He hopped onto the tractor, lowered the lift arms and adjusted the plough until it was horizontal. He put it into gear and drove forward. The plough glided along turning neat furrows as it did.

☙ ☙ ☙ ☙

Pete was watching Seamus. He was explaining what he was doing and enjoying it all.

"These pieces are heated in the forge until they reach a white-hot temperature. The surfaces to be joined must be clean and we will add flux to prevent oxidation and ensure a clean weld. The pieces will then be hammered together creating a metallurgical bond as the molecules of the steel are fused.

For jobs like the modification of old machinery we would be wise to drill or punch holes in the steel pieces first. Then place a red-hot rivet into the hole and hammer it to create a strong mechanical bond as it cools and contracts."

"I'm glad you came," Pete said. Seamus wasn't used to praise, and Pete could see it.

☙ ☙ ☙ ☙

Alice met Maureen on Monday morning at the park. Maureen loved the company and chatted incessantly.

She went silent when Alice said they hoped to leave on Thursday.

"Are you coming with us?" she asked her.

"God. I'm so nervous," Maureen replied and after a prolonged pause added that she would join them.

"Where will I meet you?"

"Right here," Alice told her. "As early as you can get here but wait until they have left."

☙ ☙ ☙ ☙

Mol was home and was reading through new legislation that had been passed by the British government. It proposed the partition of

Ireland into Northern Ireland and Southern Ireland, each with its own parliament.

Eve came in. "Hello Mol," she said. "You are a stranger around here."

Mol laughed and said, "I feel like a stranger. Joe certainly thinks I am."

"I wanted to talk to you about something."

"Go ahead sure," Mol said.

"Coleman wanted me to tell you that the RIC has got hold of intelligence that concerns insurgents being sheltered on Inis Meáin."

"What are they planning, does he know?" Mol asked, concerned.

"They are not going across. They are going to watch out for strangers. They watch that the same people come and go, but anyone else will be arrested."

"Thanks," Mol said.

༄ ༄ ༄ ༄

Pat had driven the bishop to an important meeting of the bishops of Ireland, in Limerick.

The bishops were gathering to respond to escalating violence and increasing civilian suffering.

During this meeting,

they issued a joint pastoral letter urging an end to violent reprisals and acts of terror.

The letter called on parishioners to pray for peace and to strive for justice in a manner consistent with Christian teaching. The bishops expressed solidarity with the Irish people while urging them to avoid actions that could lead to further violence or moral compromise.

Pat was listening to the other drivers. There was great support for the drive towards the independence they believed was coming.

John Joe McCarthy was one man that was spoken about with respect. He was able to gain silence whenever he spoke or was asked a question. He definitely knew stuff, Pat was sure.

"Collins and Dev are kept in safe houses," he was answering another man. "They'll never find them. They are both attending a meeting next Tuesday at Croke Park. The British won't go back there after what happened you see. Clever men."

John Joe was one of Michael Collins's men, he supplied minute detail to the intelligence unit.

They frequently intercepted British communications and identified informants.

John Joe and an army of likewise men and women had assisted in foiling British attempts to capture key IRA leaders.

John Joe was a master at letting strangers believe he was a mouthpiece, spilling details that could get men or women executed when in fact he and the numerous others had thwarted efforts to capture the leaders due to timely warnings from the network.

John Joe had one eye on Pat. He noticed how he said nothing but was listening to everything.

"Where are you from?" he suddenly asked Pat. "Ahh, Clifton," Pat replied.

"I know it," John Joe said. "There was an ambush there on the RIC station a few years back."

"There was," said Pat.

Would this be his turn to get noticed by the men around him? They were all looking at him now.

"Ya, I was actually involved in that. We killed eight of them."

John Joe looked at him closely. "Pat, you say. What is your family name?"

"Flaherty," Pat replied.

That was all he needed to say. Pat suddenly felt stripped bare.

The subject was changed to the weather.

⚘ ⚘ ⚘ ⚘

Jimmy had walked from the park to the port and it had taken him an hour and twenty minutes.

That left plenty of time to get tickets and board the ship. Today they would all walk that journey but with fear in their hearts, he believed.

Jimmy decided to go directly without Alice, James and Maureen if she didn't change her mind. It would be less noticeable, two ladies and a young boy, than four of them. Kathleen thought of everything, he said to himself.

Kathleen had suggested to Jimmy not to say to Gus at the garage anything about where he was going. "Just say a family matter. The less anybody knows the better."

Jimmy had on the bishop's old suit that Kathleen had pulled from the wardrobe and he looked smart.

"You will be treated like a gentleman," Kathleen told him, "make sure you walk and act like one."

They had laughed at Jimmy acting like a gentleman, but Kathleen said all those details are important.

The more she said, the more nervous they got.

"Alice, you will walk and act like a lady. Maureen will be minding James. Make sure your child is not called one name or the other. You don't want to raise suspicion with a simple mistake like that. Call him his by proper name, James. Carry a teddy bear and let the bear be called Zach."

"You are wasted working for the bishop," Alice said. "The things you think of."

"Where are ye going?" Kathleen continued. "Where are ye coming from? All these answers must be the same from all of you and spoken with confidence."

"Have you answers to those questions?" Jimmy asked her.

"Well, let's answer them now," she said.

"You were here on holiday to visit."

"We don't know anybody," Jimmy and Alice, both, said.

"Alright, you just came on holiday to see someplace new."

"You are going to Europe now? Where is the ship going to?"

"Liverpool, but stopping in Cork," Jimmy told her.

"Well, say Liverpool if anyone asks. Now you both need to give the same answers all the time.

Alice, you give all this detail to Maureen in a story, don't give her lots to remember or she might panic. James will be excited and that will be good. The last thing you want is for him to start crying for his mammy or daddy. Keep him occupied with games or other children. Having Maureen with ye could be the saviour. Don't do anything to bring attention to yourselves.

"Now, don't write to me, forget I exist. Same with Maureen. No letters.

"You all will just vanish. When you get home it will be a different story but the same. Don't draw attention by announcing that you have your son back. Keep him at home. Don't take him to mass or any other outing there, he will be noticed as being back. Keep him in your close family circle. One mistake, and we could all be in serious trouble.

"Make up a little song and get James to sing it with you.

My name is James

And this is Zach

We both go to school

And we both come back.

Something simple to get him comfortable with his name."

Jimmy and Alice were in awe of this girl's cleverness.

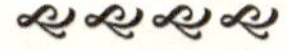

Now Alice was waiting for her son and Maureen. She was trembling with fear. Then she saw them coming. Walking a bit too quickly she thought, and she realised that she had taken in the need for normal behaviour at all times. She stood up and greeted them with a cheerful tone. "How lovely to see you. Shall we go for a walk?"

Maureen hadn't even spoken yet.

Alice continued, "And isn't it a beautiful day? We are going to have such a lovely day together.

Here, I got you a little present." She handed James a teddy bear. "Zach is his name."

"That's my name too," James said.

"You can be James for today," Alice said. "We can make up songs about you and your new friend."

As they walked along Alice sang,

"My name is James,

And this is Zach.

We are going to fly away,

And never come back."

ରେ ରେ ରେ ରେ

John Joe reported into his team in Kildare. "I have suspicions about a fellow in Clifton," he started.

"Pat Flaherty is the name."

There were clicking noises around the room followed by paper shuffling.

"Yes, I have him here," a lady called from the other side of the room. "We had him in our sights a while back, but word had come to leave him be. He is the brother of none other than Mol Flaherty."

A murmur went around the room at this revelation.

"He was a soaker," John Joe said, clearly listening to everything that was being said. "I planted a dummy seed, a meeting in Croke Park that

Connolly and Dev would be attending on Tuesday next. We will watch and see if there is a raid."

೪ ೪ ೪ ೪

Pete was fascinated with Seamus. He was a craftsman no doubt.

What Pete had attempted was crude to say the least. "When we paint the modified implements, they will look splendid."

Connor was pleased but concerned that the uptake in the sales of tractors was very slow. He was determined to overcome his concerns and proceed. An Overtime Tractor that had been manufactured in America was delivered and this brought another flurry of keen interest and enthusiasm to the yard, but no buyer.

೪ ೪ ೪ ೪

Alice could smell the sea water.

She had carried James for the last couple of miles and was puffing hard. Now the smell gave her strength. She put James down so she could catch her breath and tidy herself up before the walked the last bit. Maureen had stayed silent for nearly all the walk, now she was chatting to James. "Isn't this exciting?" James was keen to get to where this great adventure was. So, they set off again. Jimmy was waiting for them and took Maureen's bag off her.

"I have the tickets," he said.

"Hello Ja…," he nearly slipped up.

"Hello young man," he said instead.

There was a queue formed, and they joined in. Slowly they moved forward and eventually they reached the checking area. "Tickets," the man said. Jimmy handed him the tickets and was about to speak when he remembered what Kathleen had said. Act like a gentleman.

So, he kept his chat to himself.

The tickets were stamped and handed back; the man looked past Jimmy for the next passengers.

They were on. The walked up the gangway and onto the deck. In unison they all walked to the rail to see if there was anyone running and looking for them.

≈ ≈ ≈ ≈

John Joe and some of his team watched the Croke Park entrance from a distance. One of them had a sweeping brush and dustcart and was busy sweeping up leaves. Another was repairing a lamp post. John Joe was cleaning windows when all of a sudden armoured vehicles descended from every direction. The raid lasted for over an hour. By the time they were ready to leave, John Joe and his comrades had slowly drifted away.

Mol was summoned to a meeting and the news was broken to her.

She was disbelieving that he had turned back to his old ways. "I am stupid," she said, "I really thought he had learned his lesson. Right, no room for sentiment. It was most likely him that heard about the islands. Let me think about this. Meanwhile I will put two men watching him. Denny and Kieran are sleepers in the area adjacent to where he works. I will set them the task of watching and if necessary, feed him some dud information."

≈ ≈ ≈ ≈

The bunk was small for the four of them, but they were moving. It seemed like an age passed before the last trickle of passengers walked up the gangway.

Eventually a rumbling could be heard and Jimmy said, "That is the engine starting."

'We are moving at last,' they thought.

"Remember everything Kathleen told us," Alice said to Jimmy. "We must stick to the plan."

Jimmy asked Maureen if she was looking forward to going dancing every weekend. That lifted the mood. "I will get a new dress," she said.

≈ ≈ ≈ ≈

Denny and his brother Kieran received the instructions.

"It's that bloody Pat Flaherty again," Denny said. "We should have put him out to grass long ago."

Denny asked Kieran if he knew anything about the servant girl that lived in the bishop's house.

"Yes, Kieran, her name is Treasa Joyce. They are the Joyce's from Leitir Móir."

"Find out as much as you can about her. If you can get her on her own, give her the talk, the one about loose chat. Tell her if she speaks to yer man again her family will be history."

Denny looked over the location of the bishop's house.

He picked a shed full of turf which was close to the road. He clambered up on top of the turf and made a nest for himself. He removed a few sods so that he could watch. For a day and a half watching there was no movement. He climbed down and walked back to see his brother.

"Did you see her yet?"

"No," was the reply.

"Plant a seed when you do. I need to see what he does with it."

Denny took his bicycle with him and returned to his vantage spot.

Later, Kieran was in the village nearby chatting to the local merchants. When he came to the greengrocer he started to make polite conversation.

"Sure, the bishop's house must keep ye busy," he said. "Ahh, yer wan would buy very little, too expensive is her favourite line." They chatted for ages and then the grocer said, "You watch, here she comes now."

Treasa had collected carrots, parsnips and potatoes when Kieran stepped in front of her. "Hello miss," he said.

"Get out of my way," she replied.

"You have a loose tongue, so you have. You know loose talk costs lives."

She was about to say something, but the next sentence stopped her.

"Your father and mother live over in Leitir Móir. Shame if anything bad was to happen to them.

Now, you listen. You will not speak to Pat Flaherty except for one message - Guns are being landed tonight at Dublin port. Remember, not another word. Loose talk," he said as he walked away.

Treasa rushed back and decided to write down what he said on a piece of paper. She wouldn't speak to him again.

At the bottom of the note she wrote down that she had overheard His Grace on the telephone.

She went out and handed him the note.

Pat studied the piece of paper and wondered why she had given it to him. He decided to confront her about it. He went to the scullery door and knocked.

When she opened it, he saw annoyance on her face. "Why have you given me this?" he demanded.

She was clearly stuck for words.

"I'm getting him his tea," she said. "I will tell you later. I like you and I don't want anything to happen to you, that's all."

She closed the door. Pat went back to the shed. Strange that, he thought, she has a funny way of showing it. He started the car and set off.

Denny watched as he drove by.

He climbed down again and set off after the motor car.

Pat carefully drove around the deep ruts in the road and watched people turn to watch the big car.

'Wasn't he a fine fella?' he grinned as he drove on.

Bloody carts are a nuisance, he muttered as he had to slow down to crawl speed and wait for them to pull into a hedge less piece of barren wet ground to let him pass.

He drove into Clifton and turned towards the RIC station. He stopped and got out of the car and started walking up the roadway. As he got near, he put something into the post box and immediately crossed the road and down into Connor Flaherty's garage. Pete, Connor and Seamus were trying to bend a piece of steel when Pat spoke. Connor muttered 'hello' back but Pete and Seamus were too busy for chitchat.

"I'll be off so," Pat said.

Then Pete stopped and straightened himself, "What hurry is on ya?" he asked. "Will ya run out and tell your mother that Seamus will be stopping for his supper? Bring her in a lock of spuds, there's a good man," he said.

Pat left and felt he was always the odd job man. Did his father not see him all dressed in his best clothes? Bring in a lock of spuds? I have better things to do. He would go and give his mother the message anyway.

"Hello mammy," he said as he entered the kitchen. Kate was sitting, nursing baby Laura.

"Hello son," she replied.

"Daddy said Seamus is stopping for supper."

"Ahh. Will you fetch me in a few spuds so I can have them washed and boiled?"

He grabbed a bucket and did his bidding.

He recalled the event with Jimmy in this very spot.

Denny watched from a distance.

⁋⁋⁋⁋

Jimmy, Alice, Maureen and James were two days away. The five days so far had all of them being sick. James was the worst; he clung on to Alice feeling totally miserable. She believed that he had never had this affection since he was taken from her.

Maureen was delighted that it wasn't she that he was clinging to.

The teddy bear was held close to James all the time and Jimmy kept asking if Zach was feeling sick too. James seemed content that he was constantly being called James and his teddy bear was Zach. Kathleen again. That clever girl.

They decided to go up to the deck to get fresh air and hopefully try and shake off the sickly feeling.

They travelled in two groups rather than one bigger more noticeable one. They sat together on a bench and breathed in the sea air.

Jimmy nudged Alice, "Look," he whispered. A priest was standing alone dressed in his cassock.

"I wonder where he was off to?" he said. Alice stood up and took James back to the cabin.

Jimmy watched the priest. How could they do it? He wondered. What gratification could they get? Causing so much suffering with their actions.

And yet they maintain such power over people. He was tempted to casually walk over and start a conversation with him. He decided he would.

"Hello father," he said.

"Bless you my son," the priest replied.

"Fine day."

"It is."

"Are you off on your holidays?" Jimmy asked.

"I am returning from church business. And you?"

"Oh, the same," Jimmy replied. "Motor car business."

"How nice," the priest said.

"Am I permitted to ask what sort of church business?" Jimmy enquired.

"Well now, we have to meet and discuss matters of the Church, you see."

Jimmy was thinking how easy it would be to knock him overboard.

"And your motor car business, what makes you go all that way?"

"Well," Jimmy said confidently, "there are new innovations happening all the time, all over the world. I go where ever there is a new innovation and bring it home so that we can all benefit from it."

"I see you are very interested in this profession."

"I am. Transportation of people is my business you might say," Jimmy said. He watched his reaction.

"Interesting," the priest said.

Jimmy felt he better say no more.

As he turned to walk away the priest spoke, "How far did you think you would get?"

"Pardon," Jimmy said.

"I know all about your little scheme. I will hand you in at the port and return with the child."

Jimmy was flabbergasted. He had been watching us and not the other way around.

"My bishop had correspondence from your Father Michael. He informed him that you most likely would travel to America to try and find the child you gave up for adoption."

Jimmy and the priest were leaning on the rail looking back towards America. Jimmy was angry now. He turned his back and leant against the rail this time.

The priest was saying he had followed the girl Maureen and her accomplice with the child all morning to see where they were going. "I had unfortunately been unable to get my bishop on the telephone because he was out on business, his servant took my message that I was following you onto the ship."

Jimmy thought, Kathleen again. She has been our guardian angel all the time, even now.

It was getting cool, and most people were returning to their cabins.

Jimmy got his right leg in between the bottom rail and the priest. He waited a second or two and when nobody was looking their direction and with a quick sweep of his leg the priest went tumbling. A short scream came but nobody noticed.

Jimmy turned around again and scanned the water. He couldn't see him.

It was all going so well, he thought.

Possession, he said to himself. We have our child and soon we will have him in our country.

Our country, he thought about that.

It was our country after all that allowed this to happen. Well, not again. I will do whatever it takes to protect my little family, Jimmy thought to himself.

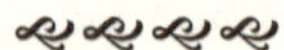

Denny reported back that the dud information fed to Pat Flaherty was delivered to the RIC station in Clifton. "We have a man there," Denny was informed. "See Coleman Casey, let him know, he will intercept any information passed until we deal with Flaherty."

Mol was home in the kitchen.

When her father and brother Connor finished their supper, Mol said, "He is at it again."

There was silence.

"He is running to the RIC with information about insurgents."

"He is going to get himself killed one of these days for sure," Pete said.

"Why?" Connor said with disbelief. "What is wrong with that lad. He bluffed us with his lies."

"He will have to disappear I'm afraid," Mol said.

"We did try by sending him away that time."

They could see Ireland. They were so excited.

Alice said, "Please act normal. We are nearly home."

A young man spoke to Maureen. She was shy and they started talking.

Jimmy looked closely at him. He is another, he thought. Jimmy grabbed him by the arm and pulled him away.

"Who are you?" he asked.

"Jesus," the lad said, "I only said hello."

"Why her?"

"Jesus, I was just being friendly."

"Where are you going?"

"I'm going home. I went like all the lads to America but I didn't like it. It's all digging and knocking down buildings. I didn't like it. What did you expect? I sold produce to the people on Achill island. I didn't want to be tattie hoker," he said. "So I went off to America."

"What on God's earth are tattie hokers?" Jimmy asked him.

"Gangs that go off to Scotland and pick spuds."

"Are you connected to the church?"

"Not connected, no. But I go to mass like everyone else."

"Are you any good at selling stuff?" Jimmy asked. He wanted to be nice to the lad now because he felt he had misunderstood him.

"Come back and chat away to Maureen. Do you like dancing? Maureen loves dancing. And, if you are any good at selling come to Clifton and find Connor Flaherty's garage."

"Hello again," the lad said to Maureen. "My name is John. Your brother tells me you like dancing."

❧ ❧ ❧ ❧

The engine slowed and the ship inched into dock. Maureen was entranced with John. Jimmy and Alice smiled at her happiness just being a young girl living her life.

John looked to be taking her bag. Was he offering to carry it for her or was there more to it?

Jimmy was nervous. Oh God. Will ye just drop the gangplank and let us off. They could swim the last bit, he thought. He was beside himself with worry.

He thought about the priest. His conscience was clear, he told himself. His family was what was important.

The gangplank was at last secured. They started to move towards it. John and Maureen were laughing at something he had said. As they stepped onto the gangplank all the emotions came. Alice had tears streaming down her face. Jimmy had a lump in his throat. Alice noticed and pulled him close. "Let's keep ourselves looking important now, so we don't draw attention."

"Where are you going sir?" Jimmy was asked. "Galway," he replied.

"Train station that way, sir."

They walked out through and hugged each other tightly.

❧ ❧ ❧ ❧

Pat sat at the table and watched Treasa. He was waiting for his breakfast. "You are a queer hawk," he told her.

"Why didn't you tell me that you liked me?"

"Ah sure, we are all different. But in any case, don't worry, I have met a boy now. 'Twas at the céili the other night."

She was the worst liar ever, he said to himself.

A note left in the box where he collected his pay stated that the last two pieces of information reaped nothing.

A waste of valuable resources. *I might not be the cleverest he thought but I'm not stupid either, Pat thought.*

But she said in her note she had overheard it on the telephone. That's possibly true, but why tell me? Pat thought to himself.

He felt uneasy.

☙☙☙☙

Jimmy said to Alice that the walk from the train station would let everyone see them with James.

"If we could telephone Connor," he said, "he might know how to help."

"Leave it to me," Connor said on the telephone. "What time is your train?"

Father Michael had just arrived in Connor's yard when Pete had told him that the telephone was ringing. Now he went back to see what he wanted. "I have no use for the motor car," he told Connor.

"Neither have I," Connor replied. "Sales are very slow. Nobody is buying anything. It's the forge that is keeping us going."

"I understand I will not get what it is worth he said, will you make me an offer for it."

"I will give you ten pounds for it if I can scrape that much together," Connor said.

Father Michael nearly dropped. "Ten pounds?" he said.

He stood for a long moment and then said, "Very well."

Connor paid him and he left with a sour face.

☙☙☙☙

It was the first time James had been on a train. He stood up looking out the window for the entire journey. When they arrived, Connor was waiting for them.

He placed Alice and Maureen in the back with James between them. Jimmy sat in the front alongside Connor. "You will have to play a hide game with him so that nobody sees him. That's all I could think of," he told Jimmy.

They met only horse drawn carts and people on bicycles on their way home. When they pulled up at the house, Kate and Pete were outside to greet them. There was wonderful excitement and conversation all about James.

            ❧ ❧ ❧ ❧

Father Michael had four large suitcases already packed. He had asked his bishop for more detail about his reassignment to the islands. "I will arrange that for you," he told him.

            ❧ ❧ ❧ ❧

Word had reached the islands that the RIC were watching the comings and goings.

They were looking for strangers.

            ❧ ❧ ❧ ❧

Coleman went to see the bishop. Treasa showed him into the waiting room.

"He will see you in a moment or two," she told him.

"Yes, Constable, how can I be of assistance?" the bishop asked Coleman.

"You are employing a dangerous individual," Coleman started. "He plays both sides.

Informer to the RIC and a willing participant carrying out atrocities for the other. Of course, you may or may not be aware of this. However, you are in grave danger. Both sides believe that you in fact could be a major player in the IRA."

The bishop was ashen faced.

"There are two things I want. One, Father Michael is going to the islands."

"Yes," the bishop said, "that's correct."

"Arrange for your man to take him. There is a small boat waiting for them at the quay tomorrow night. Your man will row the boat himself."

"And the second thing you want?"

"I would advise you to run for your life. If one side doesn't get you the other will."

Coleman stood up, turned, and left.

He was pleased with himself. He had followed Mol's instructions as she had outlined them.

The bishop calmly got up and went to see Pat.

"You will take Father Michael to Inis Méain tomorrow evening, there is a boat waiting there for you. You row him out and when you return there will be an extra twenty pounds here for you."

"Thank you, Your Grace," is all he could think to say. Twenty pounds. That's a fortune. He wanted rid of that priest pretty bad, Pat thought.

ৰৰৰৰ

Connor and Sarah were walking along the beach when he suddenly stopped and got down on one knee.

"Will you be my wife, Sarah?"

She smiled at him and said, "Yes."

ৰৰৰৰ

James kept looking at baby Laura.

"Why doesn't she talk?" he asked. "Why can't she play? What happened to her hair, did the wind blow it off."

The questions were endless.

Kate was thrilled that they were back.

Pete and Jimmy talked incessantly about all things to do with cars, tractors and machinery.

ৰৰৰৰ

Pat thought about what he would do with the money. He would treat himself. *Tomorrow I will make a plan, Pat decided.*

ৰৰৰৰ

Father Michael was still packing belongings into cases when Pat Flaherty walked in. "Are you ready?" he asked.

"What do you mean?" Father Michael asked.

"I am taking you across now."

"You?" Father Michael asked.

"Don't tell me you are bringing all them cases."

"Of course, they are my vestments and personal items."

Pat lifted a case in each hand and put them in the luggage compartment of the car. Father Michael appeared with two more. They set off for the pier.

∾∾∾∾

The bishop had thought about what to do. He decided to go for a walk. It would help him think.

∾∾∾∾

Pat placed two cases at either end and sat opposite Father Michael.

"Get out and push us off," Pat said. "I have the oars; I can't do it."

The priest got out again begrudgingly. He got his feet wet and was furious.

Pat rowed out with great difficulty until they were out of sight.

∾∾∾∾

The bishop walked along the cliff edge and couldn't face the thought of interrogation and what might come to light.

A quick sidestep took him over the edge and the long drop to the water below.

∾∾∾∾

Pat and Father Michael's boat was washed ashore the following morning.

Three bodies were washed ashore in the following days.

∾ ∾ ∾ ∾

Kate was sitting cradling baby Laura when Pete told her the news. She looked up into his eyes and said, "We will have better days."